Eastover Treasures

Published by Blue Dragon Publishing, LLC
Williamsburg, VA
www.BlueDragonPublishing.com
Copyright © 2021 by Dawn Brotherton

ISBN 978-1-939696-68-7 (paperback)
ISBN 978-1-939696-67-0 (ePub)

Library of Congress Control Number: 2021937720

Cover by Hakm Bin Ahmad

Printed in the U.S.A

21 22 23 24 25   1 2 3 4 5 6 7

Eastover Treasures

DAWN BROTHERTON

Dawn Brotherton
10 Jul 21

Dedication

To the ladies of the Colonial Piecemakers Quilt Guild
who helped make me a better quilter.

Chapter 1

Mary's long skirts swished as she hurried into the dining area. *Where do I even begin?* she thought. James had already transported some belongings, but he left her to sort out household items. How could she decide what was worth saving and what wasn't?

If she cleared too many objects, they would suspect items were hidden and go searching. She must be selective. Opening the drawer of the buffet, she withdrew a handful of items, then opened the next drawer, slamming them shut as she moved on. She repeated this process until she had a small pile.

Brushing the loose hair off her forehead, she turned to the next room. *I don't know why he has to leave now. We are supposed to be plowing a new garden.*

Outside the window, the reins clinked as James hitched the horse to the wagon. Swiftly, she shifted her attention to the parlor and took the painting from over the mantle. A lighter rectangle was left on the wallpaper where it had been. Muttering words her mother wouldn't approve of, Mary replaced the painting. She spun to take in the rest of the space.

Everything is a treasure to me! How can James not understand that?

Mary's frustration was clouding her concentration. She needed to take a minute. She stopped in the library, admiring their collection of books. Her father was a generous man and often sent treasures he found on his trips to Philadelphia. With the fighting between the north and south, no packages had come recently. She picked up the leather-bound volume he had given her when she and James moved to Virginia.

I need to get back to my writing. Father will expect to hear all the details about country life when we travel north next.

But when will that be?

Looking around, she took a mental inventory. A drop of sweat threatened her eyes, but she wiped it away with the back of her hand. Then she heard the thunder of the boys' feet across the wood floor. They skittered into the room.

"Momma, can Frederick and I go to the river to catch frogs?" nine-year-old Thomas asked.

She put on a brave face. "What are you going to do with them once you catch them?"

"We can eat them," Frederick offered.

Thomas punched his arm. "That's foul."

"No, it's not. It's living off the land. You eat what you can catch. Isn't that right, Ma?" Frederick was only ten, but already starting to talk like his father.

She smiled at the towheaded boys. "Let's save the eating until it's necessary."

"But if those secesh take our house, we may have to live in the woods. Pa said so," Thomas insisted.

"Where did you learn that kind of language, young man?"

"Noah," both boys said together.

Mary rolled her eyes. "I'll have a talk with your brother. You may go down to the river but take a basket and bring some berries with you when you come back."

The boys were out the door before she had a chance to say anything else.

"Sarah?" Mary called.

The fourteen-year-old entered the library, carrying her

latest sampler. "Yes, Ma."

"Will you get some of the quilts from the upstairs closet and bring them down?"

"Yes, ma'am."

Mary replaced the book on the shelf and plucked out another one, placing it on the side table. Then another.

"Momma?" Sarah's voice cut through Mary's wild purge. "We aren't moving all those books, are we?"

"And why not? Books have value." Mary turned away from the shelf and took in the overflowing stacks she had subconsciously built.

Sighing, she began replacing some volumes. "Why don't you help me pick the best ten to save?"

Chapter 2

Present Day

The breeze picked up as Aury St. Clair sat on the back deck of the rustic motel checking the latest weather forecast on her phone. The hurricane had shifted again, this time moving up the east coast of Florida. There was a fifty-fifty chance the weather that accompanied a storm of that size would miss their slice of Virginia all together.

Aury held the cell phone loosely in her lap and prepared to say goodbye to the solitude she had with nature. The breeze rustled the bushes surrounding the pond, sending a ripple across the water. The frogs were especially loud. Maybe they sensed the impending storm.

The phone's buzz joined Mother Nature's song, and Aury picked it up again. The cell reception was so bad this far into the woods that she was usually bombarded with text messages that had been waiting to find her phone as soon as it could get a signal. From the porch, she at least had a bar or two.

She glanced through them, answering a few from the accounting firm she worked for. They seemed to disregard the fact that she was on vacation. She tucked it away again, rising from the picnic bench.

As Aury opened the door, she was immediately flooded with

the cacophony of sounds emanating from the women jammed into the open floor plan of the activities room. The concrete walls did little to absorb the sound, bouncing it around the hall until only emphasized syllables and harsh laughter could be discerned.

Aury slid into place behind her sewing machine, which rested on a table butted against three others. The ladies continued their banter.

"Finished with your phone sex?" Debbie asked.

"I was. Don't know about him," Aury answered, just as straight-faced.

Debbie cackled. "Guys have a harder time faking it," she said, reloading her bobbin and snapping the door closed on the casing. Her soft, gray curls framed a round face that was always quick with a smile, but it was her brightly colored sweatshirts that Aury appreciated. They usually had a quick-witted line printed on them in bold colors. Today was no different: "I'm glad no one can hear what I'm thinking" was printed in neon pink.

Pat gave Aury a speculative look. "What's the weather?"

"The hurricane is scheduled to hit the east side of Florida. They still don't know if it will turn, but it's moving fast."

Debbie shook her head. "I could be a weatherman and do a better job than those bozos."

Pat ignored her. "Do we need to consider packing up sooner than planned?" A tall woman with a dry sense of humor, Pat's imposing nature hid her inner spunk. It had taken a while for Aury to figure her out. Thankfully, Pat saved her sharpest retorts for Debbie.

"No way," Linda said from the next table. "I paid for six days, and I'm going to use all six." The hum of her machine charged over the fabric in a practiced clip. "My husband would never let me get this much done at home. I'm taking advantage of the getaway."

Aury turned her gaze to the sunlight streaming through the

windows. "Looks like another beautiful day."

"You just never know with these storm patterns," Suzanne commented from across the table. "Hurricanes are fickle." She stood from her machine and limped toward the ironing board.

Aury tried to focus on one of the many projects she brought with her for this quilting retreat. She had been looking forward to it for so long, but now the projects were overwhelming, and she had trouble concentrating.

"Sam said he thinks we should head back early in case they shut the ferry down," Carla added. "Taking the twenty-minute ferry will be a lot better than the extra hour it would take if we had to go up toward Richmond and back down the peninsula."

She didn't sound worried, though. At least twenty years older than Aury and six inches shorter, Carla was a sweet soul with a positive attitude. She'd find the bright spot in the toughest situation.

"If it comes down to it, we'll close up shop. Anyone can leave whenever they want if they're nervous." Aury had spent months planning this retreat. She would hate for the weather to mess it up.

She looked around the room at the fifteen heads bent over their sewing machines and projects in various stages. Aury knew she needed to get some work done. When she got home, there would be many other projects that drew her attention away from her quilting. She wanted to get her entry for the Mid-Atlantic Quilt Festival completed before the week-long retreat ended.

At thirty-eight years old, Aury was one of the youngest in the room. Reconnecting with her grandmother through her quilting had proven a useful hobby to distract her from the what-might-have-beens that kept her awake at night. After her parents had died in a car crash four years ago, she had been wracked with guilt. They had been on their way to visit her because she was upset after yet-another argument with her husband. They drove through the night instead of waiting until the next day. A drunk driver crossed the centerline and ended their lives upon impact.

Even with her grandmother's constant assurances that it

wasn't her fault, Aury still felt responsible. And her husband gave her no emotional support. She had followed him to Williamsburg when he was offered a job, more to be near her grandmother but also as a last chance to make their marriage work. It ended less than a year later.

Now her grandmother was her best friend, and she loved spending time with her. Liza St. Clair had taught her to sew when Aury was only eight years old. They had made clothes and quilts for dolls when Aury visited on vacations. It wasn't until visiting a quilt show that Aury began to value quilting as an art, not as a necessity.

Aury leaned down to search through her fabric bag as a pretense to hide her welled-up eyes from the ladies at her table. Thinking of her grandmother stuck in the rehab hospital broke her heart. Liza was spry for eighty-one and would take on most challenges. It would be unfair to be taken out by the flu. Aury had tried to find someone else to take over the retreat so she could stay and care for her, but the old lady insisted she go. She said Aury would do more good there than at her bedside.

Chapter 3

The sun shone through the windows the next morning, lighting up the inside of her eyelids as Aury rolled over. She fought the urge to turn away from the light, but her mind started processing the next steps in her quilt. Rubbing her tired eyes, she relished in the quiet of the wooden motel that was her home for a few more days.

The layout of the Eastover Retreat Center was beautiful. The motel had sleeping quarters stretched out on either side, with a multipurpose space in the middle where they gathered to quilt. Although all the individual units had doors that opened to the outside rather than into a hallway, the path to the sewing area was under cover. It was a quick jaunt back and forth if something was forgotten.

Another upside was the parking directly outside the bedroom doors made unloading and loading a breeze. The quilters had a short walk past the lake to the dining hall where they were served lunch and dinner. Everyone commented how wonderful it was not to have to cook. They ate breakfast on their own whenever they drifted in.

Aury loved the idea of not waking to an alarm clock and took her time getting up. Eventually, the call of her sewing machine got her motivated. She slipped on a pair of flannel pajama pants, stuck her feet into old tennis shoes, and looked into the mirror.

Pulling her dark hair into a messy bun, she declared herself presentable—at least for this group.

"Morning, all," she said to the earlier risers, already engrossed in their projects. Some raised their heads in greeting, but most simply called out a hello over the whirring of the machines.

She went straight to the kitchen that took up a corner of the multipurpose room. Thankfully, someone had already brewed a pot of coffee. Aury filled a cup and wandered to her table where she stopped to stare at the mobile quilt wall hanging by sticky hooks behind her workstation. The bedsheet-sized, felt cloth was invaluable for gripping the cut triangle and square pieces of cotton to envision how the quilt would appear once sewn together. The ease of removing and rearranging the pieces made it one of Aury's best quilting investments.

"You finished a lot last night," Debbie commented.

"I'm a night owl. I think I got most of this done between midnight and three in the morning."

"That's because you didn't have Debbie yacking at you." Pat tossed a crumpled-up napkin at her friend.

Debbie screwed up her face. "Bite me."

"Seriously, see what I mean? How can we get anything done with that in the background?"

Carla came in through the door. "Looks like the rain is going to hit us today. The wind has really started blowing." As if to emphasize her words, a gust caught the door and slammed it behind her. Everyone jumped.

"Sorry," she said.

Quiet laughter rippled through the women as they shook off their nervousness.

"What time is lunch?" Aury asked.

Linda looked up from her work. "You just got here. I think you need to get some work done before you can eat."

Suzanne raised an eyebrow. "Lunch is served at noon, just like every other day. You set up the retreat. Can't you remember the schedule?"

Aury checked her watch. "Guess I still have time for breakfast."

She wandered to the kitchen, stopping to check out the creativity of her fellow guild members along the way. The best part about this retreat was picking up pointers from all the ladies who had been doing this so much longer than she had.

After she finished her cereal, Aury poured herself another cup of coffee and returned to her table.

Sorting through her boxes of scrap fabric, she tried to decide what could be repurposed. From larger pieces of material, she cut five-inch squares. For smaller pieces, she selected templates to make different shapes for future quilts.

"Lunchtime!" Nancy called.

Aury looked up, surprised that three hours had slipped by. She had worked through a sizable pile and would be ready to start sewing when they returned.

She ensured her machine was off and unplugged her iron. Ladies grabbed sweaters off their chairs, readying to leave. As Aury stepped onto the porch, the wind cut through her pajama bottoms. Sheepishly, she realized she still hadn't showered or changed yet that morning.

"I'll meet you all over there," she told Debbie and Pat as they started down the path that led to the dining hall.

Aury ran to her room, changed into jeans, and threw on a sweatshirt. She brushed her teeth and pulled her long hair into a sloppy ponytail. She decided boots would be a better choice for the walk alongside the lake, just in case the threatening rain started.

She hustled down the path, hoping to get in the food line before people returned for seconds. As she passed the pond, the bullfrogs yelled out their protest, seconded by the cicadas and other wildlife. Under normal circumstances, Aury would have enjoyed the solitary walk. Today, everyone was so worried about the storm that she had started to become worried, too.

This group of quilters had taken her in, encouraging her

to try new sewing techniques and expand her skills. She felt responsible for them, and she didn't want this storm to spoil their getaway.

Chapter 4

Aury grabbed her tray and settled at a table with Penny, Nancy, and Carol. Nancy had already finished eating and stared impatiently at her phone.

"What's up?" Aury asked, shoveling food in her mouth.

"This darn thing. There's no service out here."

"Haven't they ever heard of WiFi?" Penny asked.

"This is a retreat," Carol emphasized. "The idea is to leave behind electronics. No TVs, radios, or computers."

Penny stacked her empty dishes on a tray. "That's ridiculous. How are we supposed to know what's happening with the storm?"

Aury pulled out her phone, checking the bars. "I get service here, but it's weak. Guess it depends on your provider."

"What a waste," Nancy mumbled, shutting her phone off.

Just then, an old-fashioned ringtone sounded.

"Someone else has service." Aury winced, realizing that was rubbing salt in the wound for Nancy.

A few minutes later Carla stood. "That was Sam. The hurricane hit Florida as a Category Four. It's bad."

"East or west side?" someone asked.

"East. It pushed through Georgia and is headed up the coast. Lots of flooding."

"I thought it was supposed to turn out to sea," Penny said.

"That's one option. No one is sure at this point," Carla answered.

Penny looked at Aury. "Do you think we should leave?"

"Carla, did Sam say what is expected to happen to Virginia?" Aury asked.

"It'll probably turn into a tropical storm by the time it gets here. That means rain."

Linda stood and picked up her tray. "What's a little rain? We're inside most of the time anyway. What would we be doing if we went home? I have too many projects to finish here."

Others started to gather their things, feeling the pressure of the hurricane bearing down on them. Aury knew responsibilities at home would be calling to them.

Aury turned to answer Penny's question. "I'm sticking it out. I don't have anyone waiting for me, but no one will mind if you feel you need to go." She glanced around at the die-hard quilters of the group. She couldn't leave them alone. Although they were on high ground far above the river, Aury knew storms were unpredictable.

"I might take off a little early. I'm worried about what my dogs will do in the storm. They get all excited and might tear something up. My husband can't calm them down when they get all riled up," Penny said.

The ladies cleared their trays and bundled up for the walk back to the motel.

"I'm glad our rooms are close," Carol commented.

The ladies chattered on the walk, and Aury took it all in, content to be absorbing their quilting knowledge any way she could. She was awed by the collective wisdom in their small group.

The women shed their sweaters and jackets and settled into their places. Some put on their headphones, while others continued to talk about various people they knew.

"There is no way Fred is able to fix that roof," Debbie said. "He thinks he's God's gift to carpentry, but he doesn't have it in him."

"Let him try," Pat said. "What'll it cost you? He'll be outside enjoying himself, and you can hide in your sewing cave. If it doesn't work, I have the number of a handyman."

"I'll bet you do." Debbie gave an exaggerated wink.

Pat gave her a sour look and spoke to Aury. "Are you going to get anything done today?"

"No, I think I'll continue on my useless path of existence," Aury replied, clicking on her sewing machine. Ignoring the snort of laughter from Pat, Aury started lining up the strips she had cut before lunch, organizing the colors into the range she would use to assemble her rose cathedral window. This was supposed to be a project for her and her grandmother together. She wasn't sure she was up for the challenge alone.

"Stretch!" Aury called, standing from her seat an hour later.

Slowly the ladies put aside their work to humor their youngest member. Once everyone stood, Aury led the exercise. "Hands on your hips. Tilt your head and look at the ceiling. Push your hips forward." The ladies complied. "Feel the stretch in your lower back."

After a few seconds, she continued. "Slowly, come forward. All the way. Bend at the waist. Drop your hands and let them hang toward the floor."

Aury heard some moans and creaks, but no one complained. She had started this stretching regimen after one of the other ladies had mentioned how she was getting stiff from sitting in place for so long. Aury tried to think up different ways to keep the ladies from returning home with memories of sore and tired muscles. A non-sewer doesn't have an accurate perspective of what leaning over a machine all day does to a person.

"Slowly, stand. One vertebra at a time. Not too fast, you'll get a head rush."

"That's what he said," Debbie muttered under her breath, eliciting laughter from the few that stood nearby.

"Okay, now you can get to work." Aury continued to stand, twisting at the waist, then rolling her shoulders. She was ready to cut again. She picked up her fabric and moved to the taller cutting table.

A few hours later, Aury had made good progress on her quilt. She had a stack of four-patches made from the strips she had sewn together, cut, and then resewn. Her ex-husband had never understood the point of cutting something up to sew it back together.

When phrased that way, Aury could understand the confusion. He was never able to appreciate the beautiful patterns that emerged when things fell into place. Aury could lose herself in the colors of a well-made quilt.

She decided she needed to get some exercise before dinner. She shut down her machine and waved at her tablemates, letting them know she was setting out on her daily walk. She started down the path away from the road. Every day, she had tried to pick another route to explore. This time she headed toward the water.

The sky held a few dark clouds, but no rain had fallen yet. Aury didn't understand the fuss about the storm.

Shadows loomed on the path through the woods. After only a few steps under the canopy, the smell of decaying leaves and mushrooms overwhelmed Aury. Although it was late October in Virginia, all the leaves hadn't given up their hold yet.

Aury marched toward the glade a quarter mile ahead. The bright beacon of sunlight in the clearing blazed in contrast to the dappled light under the trees. The path through the woods was straight and well-maintained, and Aury found something unexplainably special about walking on a narrow strip of order between the natural spontaneity of the wilderness on either side of the path.

Ahead, she spotted a roughly hewn wooden arrow staked into the ground declaring that the path to the left led to the beach. Just the thought of water made Aury smile to herself. She wasn't much of a swimmer, but she enjoyed watching the current make its way past any obstacle in its path.

As she approached the fork in the road intent on heading to the beach, the vast, green lawn off the right fork caught her eye.

She hadn't been this way before and was surprised, once again, at how far the property stretched, with no one around for miles.

Only a few hundred feet down the path, she stopped, thrilled with the manor house that loomed in the distance. It was as if she had stepped back in time. The house was two stories, with white sideboards and four chimneys. The wooden shutters were closed, as if hiding its secrets from the world. Aury wasn't sure if that was a precaution against the storm or if the house was in a permanent state of hibernation.

From where she stood on the west side of the manor, Aury could see part of the circular driveway in the front, and the glassed-in porch on the back. The azalea bushes grew up close to the house, the pink flowers teasing the second-floor windows.

As she crept closer, Aury got another feeling. The original sense of grandeur was replaced with one of sadness and neglect. Paint was peeling from the wood siding, and the windows that weren't shuttered were so dirty they were hard to see into.

On the backside of the house facing the James River, the shutters had an extra board nailed across them to ensure compliance. Aury assumed that was more to ward off any intruders rather than the hurricane gusts coming off the river.

The grass had been mowed recently, so at a distance, the house still retained its dignity.

As Aury approached the porch, lightning flashed, and the first drops of rain splashed her face. Reluctantly, she took one last peek at the house and jogged down the path toward the motel, leaving the silent manor to face the elements alone.

Chapter 5

That night at dinner, Aury stalled until she was last in the food line. "I saw the manor house today," she commented to the gentleman behind the food counter.

"She's a beauty, isn't she?" Alan's face brightened. "Needs some TLC but is certainly holding her own."

"How old is it?

"Built in the 1880s, is my understanding," he replied, dishing up a large portion of fish and rice for Aury. "They used to rent it out, but the upkeep was too much." He handed over her plate of food.

"Any chance we could take a peek inside?"

The older man shook his head sadly. "I'm sorry, miss. It's been declared off limits. The insurance on this retreat center doesn't allow for visitors in there anymore."

"Who owns the retreat center?"

"It's been in the Henry Bell family for years. He left it to his son, Scott, but unfortunately didn't leave the money necessary to keep it running." Alan looked both ways before leaning conspiratorially toward Aury. "Don't be spreading rumors, but I don't know how much longer he can hang on."

"How sad. I assume this property would be quite profitable." Aury's curiosity grew, getting the best of her now.

The man gazed into the distance. "I'm not rightly sure. I

know Scott's mom wanted it left as a retreat center for people to get away from the city. She was the one who hired me, some forty years ago."

"What happened to her?"

"Died of cancer when Scott was a teenager." He waved his hand at her. "Go eat before that gets cold. You'll need your strength to battle the storm that's coming."

"How bad do you think it's going to get?"

"We haven't been hit up this ways in a while, but you can expect a solid drenching. Any of your ladies heading back to town tonight? If so, best git before dark."

"One or two might head out. They need to deal with things at home."

"Well, let me know soon if you need any help. We'll be off property until tomorrow night. Gotta rest on the Lord's day," Alan explained. "Don't worry. I'll bring crockpots of chili along with some cornbread over to the motel in a bit. All you'll have to do is plug them in tomorrow to heat it up, and you'll be set for a hot dinner."

"Sounds good. Thanks for looking out for us." Aury broke away to join the others.

As the ladies made their way back to the motel, the rain had slowed to a drizzle.

"This isn't so bad," Pat said. "Don't know what everyone's so worried about."

A flash of lightning followed closely by a rumble of thunder caught their attention. As if by instinct, they all picked up their pace, possibly the fastest many of them had moved in years.

By the time they reached the motel, they were drenched through. The women scattered back to their rooms to change into dry clothes.

Since she was wet anyway, Aury stripped down and climbed into a hot shower. As she stood under the water, she thought about what the man in the kitchen had told her.

The reader in her wondered if Scott's mother had died in

the manor house. It might make for a cool ghost story. And why was the family hanging on to the property if they were losing money? It was big enough; they could sell off a few parcels and still have hundreds of acres left. It was waterfront property. The Bell family could be rich.

The water turned cold quicker than it usually did. Aury supposed the other ladies had the same idea about a shower. She shut off the water and toweled off, her mind turning once again to her quilt project.

True to his word, Alan showed up in the activities room with a few crockpots full of chili they promptly put in the refrigerator for the night. He also left a pan of freshly made cornbread.

Aury smelled the melted butter drizzled over the yellow bread. "I don't think it'll make it until tomorrow."

"I didn't figure so." He went back to his car, returning with another pan still warm from the oven.

"You gotta stretch it out, though. There's fixins' for salad in the fridge, and you should have plenty of lunch meat and cheese. That pretty much cleaned out my pantry. I'll hit the store on my way in Monday morning."

"We appreciate it. You all have been wonderful to us."

"We enjoy having company out here. I know Scott loves to see this room busy like when his mom was alive."

"What does Scott do for a living?"

"He's an engineer in northern Virginia, but his dream is to be out here full time. I think he keeps the other job to make ends meet."

"Can't he just sell off some of the property to make it more manageable? Maybe get a little boost to fix up the rest of the buildings?" Aury asked.

Alan was shaking his head before Aury finished speaking. "Don't understand it myself. He won't consider breaking it up, and no way he'll walk away from it. Land's been in his family for years. His mother was researching the history before she got real sick. It's a shame. I thought she was rallying there for a while." An audible sigh escaped as his shoulders slumped and his eyes dropped.

"Well, I'm glad we still have Eastover to come to. It works perfect for our quilting retreats." Aury gestured at the room full of machines and focused ladies. "Some of these women wait for this all year."

Alan perked up. "Yes, ma'am. My own momma was a quilter. Nothing better than a blanket full of love to warm your bones. Speaking of which, I better get home before my wife makes me sleep outside for being late. You all have a wonderful night."

Chapter 6

Aury quilted late into the night. She enjoyed the energy of a room full of quilters, but she also looked forward to the solitude of watching movies on her eReader while she sewed. At this hour, everyone had turned in for the night.

Some of the women had packed up and headed home already. The vacant spaces looked strange in the midst of tables overflowing with material and various sewing paraphernalia. They were down from fifteen to ten women, and Aury wondered how many would leave in the morning.

As Aury freed her project from the sewing machine and prepared to move to the ironing board, she thought she heard a noise at the front of the hall. She held her breath in concentration.

There it was again! A scraping outside the front door. She stole toward the sound, keeping out of sight behind the kitchen wall. She couldn't imagine any of the ladies would be up, and even if they were, they would come straight into the hall, not loiter outside.

She peeked around the corner, but the lights inside were bright, making it impossible to see outside. As she struggled with what to do, she searched the closest table for a weapon. A giant pair of shears sat beside Linda's machine. Aury reached for them.

The crash against the door was followed by a stream of

incoherent words. Aury's head whipped around, catching sight of a man trying to right the toppled stack of chairs.

Her fear vanished, but her heart continued to pound in her chest. Aury approached the door expecting to see Alan and was ready to quiz him about why his wife let him come to work in the wee hours. Instead, she saw a man in his mid-thirties with dark, close-cropped hair. His tie was askew, and the sleeves of his white button-down shirt were rolled to the elbows.

She stopped short, but by then it was too late. He locked eyes with her, and for a moment, Aury was sure he looked frightened. Then he smiled and ran a hand through his hair.

He pushed the chairs aside and opened the glass door. "I'm sorry if I scared you. I didn't realize anyone was still awake. Of course, with all the racket I made, I probably woke everyone up."

Aury simply stared back, unsure what to say.

"I'm Scott." He extended his hand.

She took in the tan, muscular forearm before the name registered. She returned his handshake. "Are you the owner here?"

"I am." His grin was friendly. "I'm sorry I haven't come out to greet you all before now, but I was trying to set matters straight at home, so I could be here before the storm and batten things down."

He gestured toward the chairs. "I was going to put some things inside, so they wouldn't blow around if the wind catches them. Guess I should have waited until morning. I was still keyed up from the drive and couldn't sleep, so I thought I'd work a bit. I never have enough time to do everything I want."

Aury smiled. "I know what you mean. Obviously, or I wouldn't be sewing at," she looked at her watch, "two o'clock in the morning."

"I don't know how you can create such beautiful works of art from cloth. My mom was a quilter. She could spend hours behind her machine." A fleeting sign of sadness washed across his face.

"I totally lose myself in it. There are so many new patterns I want to try. Just looking at fabric makes me happy."

"Well, I should let you get back to it," Scott said. "I didn't mean to disturb you."

"It was a nice break, aside for the part where you scared me half to death. Are you staying for the weekend?"

"Yes, there are a lot of things to be done before the storm. You ladies may not want to be here. I can refund some of your money if you need to close up shop early."

Aury recognized the generous offer, especially in light of what Alan had told her about how hard it was to make ends meet. "I doubt that will be necessary. We're tough for a group of quilters."

He smiled at that. "Have a good night then." He tipped an imaginary hat.

Aury returned to her ironing board, lost in thought about Scott and his dilemma with the camp. She wondered if there was any way she could help.

Chapter 7

By the time Aury dragged herself into the hall the next morning, a few more tables had been vacated.

"So it's down to us seven?" she asked the room.

"It's going to be six. Sorry, I need to help my daughter prepare for the hurricane. She's seven months pregnant and trying to put boards up over her sliding glass window," one of the ladies said.

"More food for us!" Debbie cheered. "Chili is my favorite." The hum of her machine sounded like an agreement.

Aury poured a cup of coffee and wandered out to the deck. The sky was overcast but it was still bright. It was hard to envision how a hurricane could affect them out here.

"Good morning." Scott approached from the direction of the dining hall. "Did you quilt much last night?"

"A fair bit. Looks like you started early." In the daylight, Aury was able to see a few streaks of gray in Scott's hair and the faded blue of his eyes. He was wearing an old t-shirt and a pair of cargo shorts that showed off his tan features.

"Couldn't sleep. I came by earlier and met some of the ladies. They were kind enough to show me the quilts they're working on. Talented bunch you got there."

"Amazing, aren't they? Why couldn't you sleep?"

"My mind is constantly racing with what might go wrong in

this weather."

"Do you think it'll flood this high?" Aury remembered the steep drop off the cliff she had seen on her walks.

"No danger of flooding. I'm more worried about trees falling, to be honest. With all the rain, the ground becomes saturated, and heavy winds can knock them over easier."

"Is there anything you can do about it?" she asked.

"Not really. I was hoping to cut some of those big ones away from this building, but time got away from me. There's always something." He shook his head.

"I haven't checked the news this morning. What's the status of the hurricane?"

"It's supposed to swing up the coast of North Carolina, slowing down when it's over land. That should be another day or so."

"Good to know. We're down to only six of us, so please tell Alan he doesn't need to worry about any fancy food for us tomorrow. We're happy with soup and salad if that's easy for you."

"That would help us out. There's nothing left in the dining hall now except some canned food. Alan is going to do some shopping tomorrow on his way in."

They fell into a comfortable silence, watching the wind blow the treetops.

"Did you grow up here?"

Scott looked across the pond lovingly. "In a way. We didn't live here, but we spent every summer and most weekends here. Halloween was especially entertaining because of the haunted woods." His lips quirked into a grin.

"Haunted?"

"That's what my grandparents told us. Ethereal mists guarded part of the property, and we would dare each other to walk into it when it was especially thick." This time he laughed aloud.

"Once, my cousin Julie went in and ran out without her shoes. She was sure a ghost had latched onto her and her only escape was to ditch her runners. In the light of the day, we found her shoes stuck in the mud. After that, our grandparents weren't allowed to tell us scary stories anymore."

Aury watched the laugh lines crinkle around his eyes while he thought about happier times.

He shook himself as if coming out of a trance. "When my grandparents were alive, they lived in the manor house. We ran around like we owned the place."

"Do you have brothers and sisters?" Aury asked. She could picture a gaggle of kids playing hide and seek in the trees.

"Cousins, actually. On my mom's side. Dad didn't have any brothers or sisters. It would have been easier if he did."

She gave him a puzzled look. "What do you mean?"

"Oh, I don't mean to go on about myself."

"I'm interested. Really," she assured him.

Scott ran his hand across his face. "Well, when my grandparents died, they left this property to my dad. Mom wanted to turn it into a Christian retreat center and have youth groups out here. They sunk a bunch of their retirement money into the renovations, then Mom got sick." His voice hitched, and Aury looked away to give him a sense of privacy.

"The medical bills added up quickly with cancer. Mom passed, and then Dad lost all interest in this place. They say that happens a lot when two people are close. He died a year later."

"Sorry to hear about your family." Her stomach twisted with the shared pain of losing parents, but she wasn't ready to talk about the accident that claimed her parents.

"Thank you. I hope to keep going with the plans my parents had for this place, but I'm not sure I can swing it. It takes more money and energy than I have right now."

"I understand." Aury thought about the energy she had expended on keeping her marriage afloat, only to see it fall apart in the end.

"My mom was especially excited to see Eastover full of kids and families. And quilters, of course," he added with a grin.

"I'd love to see the plans someday. This is a awesome piece of property."

"Hopefully I'll have a chance to show you. For now, I better hustle back to my chores. And you need to get some sewing done. Those quilts won't make themselves."

Aury gave a little wave and headed indoors. The room was almost eerily quiet with only the few ladies that were left.

"Can we at least put on some music now?" Debbie asked. "We should be able to agree on something with six people."

"Seven," Carla corrected her.

"Ah, she don't count." Debbie indicated the lady who was packing her things. "She's deserting us."

Chapter 8

A s Aury took her usual walk before dinner, she wandered toward the manor house again. This time, she admired it from a distance, preferring to think of it as it must have been in its heyday.

Aury pictured kids of various ages running through the halls and almost heard the cry of the house matron as the kids let the screen door slam shut as they ran out to play. She smiled at her musings as she took the left fork in the path through the woods that led toward the beach.

At one time, this path was obviously tended but not in the recent past. Oyster shells littered the walkway and crunched under her feet. The leaves still hanging on to the trees overhead muffled most of the sounds except in Aury's immediate area.

Climbing over fallen tree trunks that must have been there for years, she was glad she was wearing jeans and not shorts for this adventure.

She stopped to examine how the roots of a fallen tree had dislodged what appeared to be a marker stone. Now covered with moss, the two-foot cube rested askew with one corner pointed up as if it had stopped in mid-spin. The rough-hewn edges must have been chiseled, not cut with any modern equipment.

Aury brushed at it with her hand, but the moss and dirt didn't loosen their hold easily. Wiping her hands on her pants, she continued along the trail. The downward slope made for an easy enough walk, although the roots pushing up through the groundcover were a tripping hazard.

At the edge of the woods, she stopped to take in the broad expanse of the James River. Even on this overcast day, the sight was impressive. Off on the distant shore, lights shimmered from houses tucked into the woods. With another deep breath to fill her full of happy thoughts, Aury turned to her right to continue along the riverside.

As she prepared to turn back, Aury spotted what appeared to be an opening in the foliage. A tapestry of vines hung like a curtain across what used to be a path. Finding a long piece of driftwood, Aury swung at the vines, trying to loosen them from their sticky grip. They were thick and tangled, and Aury soon gave up on her adventure.

She glanced at her watch, deciding it was time to head back the way she came. The wind picked up, and the promise of spicy chili and cornbread made her stomach rumble.

The chatter of the women and the hum of machines was a welcome home as she stepped into the room, but the rhythmic pulse coming from Debbie's phone made Aury laugh. Debbie sang along with Taylor Swift, and her head bopped with the beat.

"I see you found music you all agree on."

"Agree? Who said anything about agreeing? Debbie turned on this crap, and we're stuck with it," Pat said.

"Bite me," Debbie replied without missing a beat.

Aury laughed as she stepped to the sink to wash the dirt from her hands.

Carla followed her into the kitchen, filling up a plate of snacks from the leftover assortment. "Have a nice walk?"

"It's beautiful out here. I wish we could stay longer."

"Be careful what you wish for. I hear the storm is moving faster than they thought."

"Glad I brought a lot of projects."

Most of the ladies retired early that night, leaving Aury and Carla alone at opposite ends of the hall working. Aury had her earplugs in, half-listening to the movie she had downloaded to her tablet. Carla was absorbed in her ironing.

The lights flickered, causing both women to glance up in surprise. They had just turned back to their work when the lights flickered again, then went out.

The darkness fell on them. Aury pulled at the wires in her ears. "Carla?"

"I'm still here."

"I wonder if they have a generator."

"I doubt they would for this building," Carla said.

Aury waited for her eyes to adjust to the dark but nothing happened.

"Watch out for the hot iron," Aury cautioned Carla as she got up from behind her machine. Without the sound of the sewing machine, the howling of the wind instantly became more evident.

"I guess we may as well go to sleep," Carla suggested. "Doubt we'll get anything else done tonight."

"Do you need help finding your way?" Aury held up her tablet, which was still playing on battery. The faint glow lit a few feet in front of her.

Carla moved cautiously around the table, avoiding the tripping hazards. She reached down and unplugged the iron. "Let's not take any chances." She grabbed her keys and cell phone. Her phone flashlight illuminated in her hand. "I can make it from here. Hopefully they'll have things under control in the morning."

She went out the back door as Aury moved to the front of

the hall. Her room was on the side of the building closest to the parking spots. Stopping at her table, she picked up her cell phone and turned off the tablet. Her phone was at fifty-three percent. She cursed herself for not charging it earlier in the night.

Using her phone as a flashlight, she stepped into the night. The rain came down in sheets. Large puddles had formed around the cars, indicating it had been raining for a while.

After changing into her pajamas, she slipped into bed and pulled the blankets over her shoulders, listening as the rain attacked the roof.

Chapter 9

Aury was deep in sleep when a pounding at her door brought her upright.

"Aury! Wake up! We need to get out of here!" The pounding continued.

She stumbled from her bed, flinging open the door.

Debbie was about to pound again when Aury caught her arm. "What's going on?"

"Look!" Debbie pointed toward the center of the building. In the early morning light, Aury could see a bramble of branches blocking the sidewalk.

The rain was still falling, with gusts of heavy wind pushing it under the protective covering of the sidewalk. The whoosh of the storm through the standing trees was loud. Aury was surprised she'd slept through the turmoil.

"Is anyone hurt?" she asked.

"I don't know. Pat is waking up the other half of the building. I told her we'd meet in your room."

As Aury stepped aside, allowing Debbie to enter, Carla appeared.

"Suzanne's on her way," Carla said. "She needed to grab a few things."

The woman was soaked from her run around the fallen tree. Aury went into her bathroom, returning with towels. Next, she searched the closet for extra blankets.

When Pat came in leading a very shaken Linda, Aury wrapped a blanket around her. "What happened?"

Pat guided Linda to the bed. "Quite a few trees are down on the other side of the building. One went through Linda's window. Luckily her bed was at the opposite end. No harm done."

Suzanne rushed through the door, slamming it behind her. "Damn this hurricane!" She flung her overnight bag into the corner.

Carla tossed her a damp towel. "Now what do we do?"

"I suppose we should sit tight. I think it's a good idea to all stay together," Aury said.

"I don't like the looks of the trees. They're too close. Who's to say when another one is going to fall?"

"I say it's time to give up on this retreat. Let's head home," Pat said.

"Fat chance the ferry is operating," Carla pointed out.

"Hell, I don't think most of our cars are accessible. At least three are buried in that mess out there," Suzanne said.

The women instinctively turned toward Aury. Taking a deep breath, then letting it out as slowly as she could manage, a plan began to take form.

"Has anyone tried to call for help yet?"

The women looked sheepishly at each other. Suzanne picked up her phone. "No bars."

Linda shivered. "Mine's still in my room somewhere."

"Mine too," Carla admitted.

Pat and Debbie both checked their phones, swearing in frustration at the lack of a signal.

"Mine was running low when the power went out. I shut it down to conserve the battery. It most likely doesn't have a signal either," Aury said.

A thunderous crash made the women jump and someone screamed as the ground shook.

"Now what?" Debbie cried.

Aury went to the door, opening it a crack. "Good news and

bad news." She closed it again. "The rain is letting up, but I think we just lost access to the other cars."

The six women huddled in the cramped room.

"I don't want to stay here," Linda said.

"I don't blame you," Pat said. "But where can we go?"

"What about the dining hall?" Debbie suggested.

"Walking around that lake isn't the best idea. It gets muddy at the slightest hint of rain. It's been pouring for hours," Carla said. "Who knows what shape it's in."

"But we're going to need food," Debbie said.

"Leave it to you to be thinking about your stomach at a time like this." Pat gave her an incredulous look.

"It's survival," Debbie shot back.

"Alan said the cupboards were bare," Carla reminded them. "He was going shopping on Monday."

"I'll go to our stash in the sewing room and see what I can salvage," Aury said. She emptied her suitcase on the bed.

"I'm not sure you can get to the door," Suzanne said. "The branches are awfully thick."

Aury shoved her arms into a jacket. "I'll do what I can." She pulled her boots on over bare feet and grabbed the empty suitcase.

"I'll go with you," Debbie said. "You'll need help carrying things."

"Geez, Deb, how much food do you think we need?" Pat said.

"We don't know how long we're going to be here. Better to be prepared."

Aury and Debbie stayed under the overhang as long as they could. The wind had slowed so the rain wasn't coming at them broadside anymore. Still ten feet from the front door, the heavy limbs and soggy leaves blocked their path. Aury attempted to pull the branches apart to make an opening, but there was no forgiveness in the fallen tree.

"Let's try the back door," Debbie suggested. She dashed out

into the drizzling rain, making a wide arc around the mound of twisted roots that stood almost as tall as she was.

Aury studied the second tree that had fallen across the hood of her car and protruded into the room of the woman who had vacated only the day before. She shuddered.

Following Debbie, Aury splashed through the murky morning.

As they rounded the corner, their hopes fell upon seeing the number of trees down. Even the steps to the deck were buried under foliage.

Aury picked a route around the mess. "Wait, I think we can get in here." She melded into the branches as she pushed her way to the broken window. Using the suitcase to clear the remaining glass in the frame, she stepped carefully up to the opening.

"Be careful of the glass," she warned as Debbie drew closer. Aury threw the suitcase into the room, then gingerly climbed over the sill. Reaching around, she helped Debbie through.

"Maybe we should forget this," Debbie said. "The roof could fall in."

"Wait here. I'll see if I can reach anything." Aury disappeared among the leaves and branches. When she returned, she looked like she was covered with leaf-shaped stickers. Her arms were laden with soggy boxes of snacks, and she held plastic bags in both hands. She dumped them unceremoniously into the suitcase.

"See if you can make them fit. I think I can reach the bottled water under the counter." Aury went once more into the gloom.

She appeared again, triumphant with a partial case of bottled water. "I think this is it. Everything else is soaked and not edible."

Debbie finished zipping up the suitcase. "Can you carry that? There's no room."

Debbie went through the window first, and Aury handed out the loot. Soon they were reporting to the waiting ladies.

"I grabbed dry clothes and some extra shoes from my room while you were gone," Pat said.

"I've got my bag of stuff," Suzanne offered.

"I tried to get into my room, but the door is blocked now," Carla said.

"Now what?" Linda asked.

"What about the manor house?" Aury asked.

"Manor house?" Carla asked.

"Haven't you seen it? It's past the fork in the road, farther down the trail."

"I haven't gone that far," Carla admitted. "I've been too busy sewing."

"Our machines!" Suzanne cried out. "They're going to be ruined!"

"And our projects," Linda added. "All that work for nothing."

"Fabric can be washed," Aury said. "Let's get safe first. Do you want to wait here while I check out the house?"

The gust of wind rattled the small window in Aury's room in reply. "We're going with you," Pat said. "We need to stay together."

"Does everyone have shoes at least?" Aury picked up a pair of shoes by the door and handed them to Linda. "They might be a little big but it's better than nothing."

Linda tied the sneakers tightly and stood. Aury glanced around the room for anything else they might be able to use.

"I put some of your stuff in my bag," Suzanne said. "Thought we might be able to use it later."

Aury nodded and led the ragtag group through the mist toward the fork in the road.

Chapter 10

The rain had let up by the time they entered the clearing surrounding the manor house. Aury led the way, dragging her now-soaked suitcase full of food. Carla was close behind, her arm linked through Linda's, a gesture of moral support.

Pat and Debbie carried the case of water between them, while Suzanne shifted her bag from one shoulder to the other.

"*That's* where you want us to stay?" Linda asked in dismay.

"Well, there are no trees within falling distance of it," Aury said.

"But it's all boarded up," Suzanne pointed out.

The ladies drew closer as a gust of wind tugged at their soggy clothing.

Aury passed the handle of her suitcase to Carla. "Wait here. I'll check the other side."

She took off at a slow jog. On the side of the house facing the cliff's edge, a loose board hung from the doorframe. She cautiously climbed up the mostly rotten steps to the back porch. With both hands, she gripped the loose board and tugged.

Aury lost her balance when the board buckled with much less resistance than she expected. Her right foot slammed down hard as she tried to catch herself. The soft wood gave under the pressure, and her foot sank through the deck boards.

Cursing loudly, she managed to stay on her feet. After gently freeing her foot, she used the board she had pulled from the door to test the remaining wood to find a solid place to brace her feet.

With her left hand, she shook one of the remaining two boards crisscrossing the doorway. It didn't give easily, so she created a lever with the loose board. After a few hard tugs, she was able to pry apart the barrier.

Now facing the door, she tried the doorknob, hoping for a little luck. When that didn't work, she said a quick prayer for forgiveness before using the wood to smash the door's glass pane, allowing her to reach inside.

"Are you okay?" someone called.

"Fine," she yelled. "Give me another minute."

Reaching her hand through the broken glass, she was able to unlock the bolt on the door. This time, turning the glass doorknob admitted her to the darkness inside.

Like most plantation houses, this was built to maximize air flow. Aury used the dim light to head for the door directly opposite the one she entered through, floorboards creaking under her feet. Unlocking the door, she threw it open to find her way blocked by three similar boards nailed across the frame.

The ladies were waiting for her at the foot of the porch steps. "Stand back," Aury said.

Putting her hands on either side of the frame for leverage, Aury kicked out with her right foot at the lowest of the boards. It took four solid hits before the board finally surrendered, skittering down the steps. For the middle board, Aury retrieved the plank from the back door and used it to hammer against the obstruction. The years of weather and decay assisted her with the task and soon the doorway was clear.

"Watch your step for soft spots," Aury cautioned as the women rushed up the steps, eager to be out of the wind and drizzle. Aury took the suitcase from Carla and helped the ladies inside.

"Let's see what we can find," Aury suggested. "Be careful

though. Alan said it's been boarded up for a while, so they haven't done any maintenance. I don't know what kind of shape it's in."

The ladies split up in groups of two and explored the house. Aury and Carla took the lower floor on the east side. The first room they entered was furnished to seat twelve comfortably at a feast. The long wooden table was complete with a candelabra in the center resting atop a quilted table runner. The thin layer of dust was the only telltale sign that dinner hadn't been served in a long time.

A doorway off to their left exposed a kitchen, relatively small for the size of the house. The appliances were at least twenty years old but looked serviceable. Aury searched the pantry while Carla opened and closed cupboards.

"There's some canned goods in here," Aury said.

"I found some baking supplies but not sure how much extra protein has gotten into them." Carla held up a bag of sugar, drilled through the sides where the bugs had burrowed.

"Pass," Aury said. She turned the dial on the stovetop. A hiss escaped, but no flame. "If we can find some matches, we can heat some things up."

Carla turned the faucet on. It sputtered and spit. She shut it off. "Oh well. Without a pump, I think we're out of luck there."

"Let's go see what the others found."

They all met in the parlor. Pat peered into the fireplace. "I'm not sure if we should trust this," she said. "The flue seems to work, but who knows what's built nests in the chimney."

"We found a few beds but the quilts on them are covered with dust," Linda said.

"Let's try shaking them out," Aury suggested. "Then at least we'll have something to keep us warm. With all this rain, it's getting chilly."

A few minutes later, Linda and Debbie returned with their arms loaded with quilts. Suzanne grabbed some and the trio went to the front porch. Carla followed, carrying an old broom from the kitchen. The rain fell harder now, but the women turned their backs to the wind and set about cleaning the quilts.

While two ladies held up a quilt, Linda beat it with the flat part of the straw. Dust rose in a large puff cloud, causing all five women to cough.

Suzanne stepped away from the quilt, admiring it. "Do you see this beautiful pattern?"

Aury leaned out, trying to hold the quilt to get a better look. "It's pretty, but I can't make out the design from here."

"Trade places with me," Suzanne suggested.

Linda took the other corner, allowing Carla to also take in the whole quilt at once.

"Have you seen that pattern before?" Aury asked.

"Something about it is familiar, but I'm not sure. We'll have to ask Pat," Linda said.

The ladies went to work on the other quilts they had gathered until they were satisfied they had enough to keep them warm through the night.

Inside, Pat had a small fire going.

"I tested it with a small bundle of papers, and it seemed to be drawing fine. Figured we can start small and just watch it closely."

"Where did you get the wood?" Carla asked.

"Off the parlor there's a storage room. There's some wood but looks like it's been there a while. It'll burn quickly."

"Get out of your wet clothes—especially your shoes and socks," Aury said to the small group of women. "Wrap up in the quilts while we try to dry out the clothes a little."

"Check this out," Debbie said, pulling over a wooden rack and placing it in front of the fire. "This will be perfect for hanging your clothes on."

The women stripped down to their driest layer, draping their wet things on the rack. Then they crowded around the small fire, absorbing the heat.

Chapter 11

"A nyone know any ghost stories?" Pat asked.

"We are *not* telling ghost stories," Carla said.

"I know some dirty jokes," offered Debbie.

"No doubt," Pat said.

Linda got up and roamed over to the bookcase. "There's got to be some good reading here." She ran her finger along the spines. "Oh, look, an old photo album."

She pulled it out, handing it to Suzanne. She reached for another one. Settled in front of the fire, both ladies flipped through the pages.

"This picture was taken at the front entrance to Eastover. Must have been a while ago; the photo is black and white," Suzanne said.

Aury leaned over her shoulder. She pointed to the small numbers written in the corner of the page. "Those must be Scott's grandparents. They look so young."

"Scott who?" Linda said.

"The owner. He said he stopped by and met you all."

"Oh, him. He's a cutie." Debbie gave Aury a sidelong glance. "When did *you* meet him?"

"When he first showed up. It was late, and he was putting things away before the storm."

"So that's the real reason you stayed up so late *quilting.*"

Debbie used her hands to make air quotes.

"And why you don't get much done," Pat added.

Aury smiled but didn't bother to comment.

Suzanne flipped a few more pages. "Here's where they were building the motel."

"This album is even older," Linda said. "Some of these pictures are easily from the late eighteen-hundreds. I'll bet those are slave quarters." She indicated a small cabin where a black couple stood arm in arm. Laundry hung on a clothesline to the right of the timber-clad building, only large enough for a single room.

"What's that building?" Pat asked, pointing to a photo of the same couple standing in front of a stone structure.

Linda squinted at the small photo. "It's a church of some sort, I would think. The woman is holding flowers. Maybe a wedding. I don't remember seeing the building though. Aury, have you seen a church on your walks?"

"No. I would have remembered that."

"I wonder where it was." Linda moved nearer to the fire.

"Not so close," Debbie said, pulling her back. "All we need is for you to catch something on fire."

After entertaining themselves with the photo albums, the ladies began rummaging through the other books.

"This one looks like a diary," Aury said. She brushed her fingers across the rough leather. It was dry and brittle, flaking away in spots. Carefully, she opened the book.

The women waited in silence.

"What has you so entranced, Aury?" Pat asked.

"What? Oh, this diary starts in 1846. It's hard to make out some of the writing."

"Read it out loud," Carla said.

The ink of the flowering handwriting was faded in places.

"The date on the first page is December 1846.

"Father presented me with this gift that I

may take note of happenings in our area of the Commonwealth of Virginia as I start my life as Missus James Townsend. I am not convinced that life in this wilderness shall be worth mentioning, but I do so for the sake of my father."

Aury skipped a few pages that were stuck together. Maybe later she would be able to separate them, but she didn't want to damage anything. She continued reading aloud.

"April 1847. Our goat has produced a kid. It is a luxury to have fresh milk every day. I should like to try my hand at making cheese. At our next opportunity, I will suggest a trip into town so I may converse with the shopkeeper's wife as to the needed ingredients. How I wish I had paid more attention to the kitchen ladies in my mother's house!

"Vegetables are popping up in the garden plot out back. The ground appears to be fertile, as do I. I hope to give James a son before Christmas this year. What a joy it will be to spend the holidays with a special gift. I have not ventured to tell James yet. I want to wait until there is no question."

"I can't believe that diary is just sitting here on a shelf. It should be in a museum," Linda said.

"I wonder if Scott even knows it's here," Aury said.

The windows rattled as a gust of wind hit the house. Minutes later, the sound of heavy rainfall rose in a crescendo, then dropped slightly into a steady pounding.

"I don't know about you all, but I'm tired," Pat said, standing with a bone-cracking stretch.

The fire had died out, but Aury stirred the ashes to make sure nothing was left burning. Then she moved the heavy fire screen in front of the opening.

"I'm going to see if any of those beds are useable," Pat said.

The other ladies agreed and soon had split off to the various bedrooms, still wrapped in their quilts.

Chapter 12

A ury rolled herself out of bed early. Carla was asleep in the twin bed on the other side of the room. Excited to get back to the diary, Aury padded down the stairs. She considered rekindling the fire but decided they should save their dry firewood in case they were there that evening. They might need it for light as well as heat.

Wrapping herself in the soft fabric of the worn quilt she had pulled from her bed, she settled near a window to read.

September 6, 1861

> *News reached us today that President Jefferson Davis has moved to Richmond. That is a mere day's ride away!*
>
> *James insisted that we remove some of our prized possessions from the household and sequester them in another place on the property. He is concerned that with the fighting sure to come, we are in danger of becoming overrun.*

"Good morning."

Aury was roused from her concentration when Debbie entered.

"Are you still reading that diary?"

"It's fascinating. I'm already in the second volume."

Debbie settled on the couch and tucked her feet under her. She was also draped in a bed quilt. "Okay, give me the cliff notes version."

"Well, Mary Townsend had a rude awakening to country life. She got pregnant right away and had a little girl. That daughter died soon after birth, but then Mary had another girl, then three boys within four years." Aury's brow scrunched in concentration. "I think she had another baby who died, but then had another daughter who lived."

"That's depressing. I wouldn't want to give birth that many times."

"It was normal back then. The cool part is all the things she taught her kids. Mary educated her children herself. She had private tutors growing up, so she was well-educated. But she didn't teach them just reading, writing, and arithmetic; she taught them how to run a farm. And she taught the girls right alongside the boys. Quite forward thinking for that time period."

"What kind of farm was this?"

"At first they had a lot of lumber. They sold off lumbering rights to a timberman but kept the property. After the trees were cut, they turned some of it to crops." Aury stood and stretched.

Carla and Linda entered the room together, each wrapped warmly in the patchwork quilts. Although the colors had faded over many washings, the patterns were still strikingly beautiful.

"I don't suppose we have any coffee?" asked Linda.

"No such luck," Aury said.

"A girl can dream though."

Carla stared out the window. "Sounds like the rain has stopped at least. I wish we had some way to track the storm. Would be nice to know if it has passed and someone is coming to get us."

"Hang in there. It's not like they don't know we're here. I'm sure they'll come soon," Aury reassured her.

"They don't know trees have blocked our cars in, though. They probably figured we left by now."

"Somebody will miss us eventually."

Aury joined Carla in front of the wavy panes of glass. "I think I'll go for a walk and check out the damage. I need to move around and warm up."

As Aury picked her way through the fallen debris, her mind fell back to the diary. She had always loved scavenger hunts growing up. Her grandmother created them for when Aury visited during the summer. Aury had to collect certain items around the house and yard to win the final prize. Sometimes it was nothing more than a book, but the prize wasn't the best part anyway. It was about the search.

Aury admired the tenacity of Mary Townsend. She made a mental note to visit the library when she got back and see what else she could find about this area from that time period. An involuntary shudder ran through her. She couldn't imagine raising five kids nowadays, let alone 160 years ago.

Her foot slipped off the fallen tree she was climbing over, sending her headfirst into the branches reaching toward the sky. Unable to get her footing, she fell deeper into the maze of limbs and leaves soaked from the storm.

Irritated, she resigned herself to her undignified position. She lay face down buried in the leaves, trying to decide the best way out.

"Find anything interesting?"

Aury started at the voice. She reached down to find something solid to push against so she could get up, but only managed to bury her arms deeper into the wreckage that was once a tree.

"Here. Let me help you. You're tangled."

Scott put an arm under each of Aury's armpits and dragged her free.

"Now that's embarrassing," she said, wiping wet leaves and twigs from her arms and pants.

"Good thing you didn't see me about thirty minutes ago

when I was drowning in mud. I'm lucky I came out with my shoes on."

Aury took in Scott's mud-caked jeans and the dried smears across his face. She couldn't help but laugh.

"What happened?" she asked.

"The roads are a mess. I was making my way back here when I discovered an unusually deep puddle."

"Glad you survived. How are things looking in town?"

"There are trees down all over and no electricity in the area. The Red Cross has set up water stations throughout the county."

Aury stopped smiling. She had no idea the storm had hit so hard.

"I had a feeling you'd still be out here. You don't give the impression of being the type to quit," Scott said.

"Not just me. Some of the other ladies are here."

"Well, looks like you'll be here a while longer, unless they're up for a long hike. The dirt road from Route 610 to here is washed out as it crosses the creek. Caved in." He gestured to the fallen tree. "And you can imagine how many more traps like this lay between here and there."

Aury's stomach turned. She wasn't sure how she was going to break it to the others.

"I'm worried about you in the motel without power. We can gather blankets from the other rooms."

"Ah, about that." Aury hated to add more bad news to his day. "The hotel took quite a hit from the trees." She told Scott about their adventures in the storm and how they ended up at the manor house.

When she finished, Scott's face was drained of color. "But no one's hurt, right?"

"No, we're all fine. In need of coffee perhaps, but not hurt."

"Good." He ran his hand through his hair. Aury noticed the stubble covering his tanned face.

"I can do something about the coffee, at least. Are you up for a detour?"

Aury agreed and followed him back the way he had come.

"We have a few other cottages on the property. We usually stock them with goodies to welcome guests. Let's see what kind of shape they're in."

They picked their way down another path Aury hadn't noticed before. Trees crisscrossed the road, some holding each other up like drunken sailors. They came to a clearing in which three small cottages sat. One now sported a thick tree trunk across the roof.

"Damn," Scott said quietly. He took a deep breath and let it out slowly. "Let's see what we can find."

In the first cabin, Scott unlocked a closet filled with cleaning supplies. He pulled out empty grocery bags that were hanging on a nail.

Aury opened a bag and held it while Scott opened another cabinet, emptying the shelves of everything useful he could find. There was coffee, sugar, creamer, snack bars, peanuts, and pretzels.

A thorough search through the cabinets revealed other things previous campers had left.

Scott and Aury searched the other cabins as well and were loaded down as they headed back to the manor house.

Chapter 13

The ladies jumped up as Aury entered the room.

"Where have you been?" Deb asked.

"I come bearing gifts," Aury replied. Scott followed in behind her. "And news from the outside. Let's move into the kitchen."

The ladies crowded close behind as Aury and Scott dumped their bounty on the countertop. Debbie picked up a small bag of coffee and kissed it.

"Scott, you are my hero."

Pat snorted. "What good is that going to do you? Hard to run a coffeemaker without electricity."

Scott was rummaging around in the pantry. "Ah ha!" Triumphed, he held high an old, beat-up metal pan with a spout off one side.

"And?" Deb asked, waiting to see why he was so excited.

"This is what Grandma used to make coffee over the fire when we camped." He opened the lid. "The wire mesh is here but you may get grounds in your mug."

Debbie took it from his hands. "More fiber. It'll work."

She grabbed a few bottles of water from their stash and the bag of coffee. "Find us some mugs," she directed to no one in particular. Carla began searching the cabinets.

Linda was looking out the window. "Where's your car?"

"Miles down the road. The way is blocked, so I had to hoof it. I wanted to see if you all were still at the motel."

"Are you taking us out of here?" asked Suzanne.

Scott shook his head. "Sorry, it's a mess between here and my car, and I don't think you'd want to make that hike. It's best for me to head to town and find others to help me cut through the debris. Then we can get more vehicles closer."

"We'll have to walk quite a way though," Aury added. "The road is washed out, so they won't be able to drive down here."

"I can take a few of you now, if you feel up to the hike. Then I can return for the rest later," Scott suggested.

Aury looked at the ladies. Three of them were in their seventies, and Debbie had bad knees. She couldn't imagine them climbing over the fallen trees like she had done.

Pat must have been thinking the same thing. "Or we can just camp out until you get things cleared away."

Carla smiled. "We can rough it for a few days. I doubt things are much better on the outside."

"Scott says the power is out all over the place. The roads are in bad shape. We're so deep into the woods, the downed trees have us isolated."

"And just think, we thought the solitude here was a blessing," Linda said.

"I'm sorry, ladies," Scott said. "I'll refund your money, of course."

"What are you talking about? You didn't cause the storm," Carla said.

"This is going to make for one hell of a story at the next guild meeting," Pat chimed in.

"Good news is the hurricane has run its course and the worst of the storm is over. This area got hit with a lot of flooding and high winds though. It'll take a while to recover," Scott said.

"Come have some coffee with us," Aury offered Scott.

"No thanks. I should get moving. Why don't you all write down phone numbers of people you need me to contact when I get to town? No guarantees though. Towers are down in places, so getting through might be difficult."

Linda went to get a phone number from Deb. The others wrote their information on an old paper bag that had been wedged between the stove and the cabinet.

Aury walked with Scott out to the path leading through the woods. "Great job getting them all into the manor house," Scott said. "I owe you big for that."

"Sorry there's so much damage on your property. It'll be a mess to clean up."

Scott shrugged. "What's done is done. I'll have to see what the insurance is willing to do for me. This might be the end of Eastover."

"Don't say that," Aury said. "There has to be a way to rebuild."

"I appreciate your interest." Scott smiled. "Oh, I guess if you're staying, we should try to get the pump working. You'll need access to water to flush the toilets."

"I meant to ask you about that." Aury blushed. "We've been sneaking outside, but I'm sure we would all prefer something a little more civilized."

She followed Scott to the yard behind the house. Pushing aside some bushes, he revealed a hand pump that looked to be fairly new. "We keep this active and use it to water the plants. You just pump this handle." He demonstrated, then motioned for Aury to try. It took all her strength in both arms to pull the handle hard enough to make water flow, but after the initial murky stream, it was clear and cool.

"There are buckets by the back porch. After you use the toilet, dump water into the bowl. It'll flush on its own."

"Sounds like this isn't the first time you've had to resort to this method," Aury said with a smile.

"As you can imagine, the house wasn't built with indoor plumbing. That's why the bathrooms jut out from the sides." He pointed out the small rectangle attached off the kitchen. "It wasn't until years later that they added the indoor toilet that emptied into a chamber pot underneath the hole, outside the house. Then they finally added plumbing. When my grandparents lived here, they always had problems with the pipes, so we learned this method of flushing. Hauling water in buckets was one of our chores."

Aury laughed. "It's better than emptying chamber pots."

"Absolutely! They finally upgraded the pipes. But of course, we've lost electricity out here before which shuts down the water pump from the well, so I know the trick still works."

"Thanks for the hint. I'm sure we'll all appreciate it."

Scott wiped his hands together. "Guess I should concentrate on getting you out of here. It'll be morning before I can round up people to start clearing the road to get you out. Folks are working to clear the major roadways first. Emergency crews from Tennessee and Pennsylvania are trying to restore power. I'll bring you real food tomorrow. Will you all be okay here?"

"Sure. We're a hardy bunch. Besides, it may give us some time to find the hidden treasure."

"The what?"

"I hope you don't mind, but we've been rummaging through the old books in the library. I found diaries that must have been in your family for generations."

"Oh. I've never paid much attention to that stuff. Figured it was all junk if it's been on the shelves all this time."

"Some great-relative of yours talked about hiding valuables around the estate to keep them out of the hands of soldiers. Have you ever found anything?"

"It may be long gone by now, if it was ever there."

"Just think, maybe you'll stumble across a treasure as you rebuild, and you'll be rich after all."

Scott laughed. "Now wouldn't that be a turn of events? I better get clearing trees and leave the treasure hunting to you. Be careful."

Aury waved as he disappeared around the house and into

the woods. A shiver ran through her, and she realized she was still soaked from her fall in the wet leaves. Before going back into the house, she filled a bucket of water to carry inside.

Chapter 14

A ury joined the others in the library. The room was quiet as the ladies luxuriated in the taste of their hot coffee.

"Now what?" Deb asked.

The others turned to Aury expectantly. She peered out the window.

"Looks like it'll rain again. We'll hunker down here until Scott comes back with reinforcements."

"I'm enjoying the peace and quiet," Suzanne said, putting her feet up. "It'll be a mess at home. No one wants to clean out the refrigerator after the power has been out for a while."

"Who wants to go on a treasure hunt?" Aury asked.

"What are you going on about, girl?" Deb said.

"The diary says Mary Townsend hid things around the house to entertain her kids. Let's try to figure out where."

"I'm in," Linda agreed. "It'll at least take our minds off the weather."

Aury picked up the diary she had been reading. She flipped through the pages until she found the part she was looking for.

"*January 10, 1862. The children are restless. The weather is dreadful, and the youngest are feeling the effects of being indoors too long. It has been days since James left for town to hire more help and purchase livestock. Noah went with him, but we have heard nothing from them. I hope James gets a good price for the furniture he took to sell. He is such a skilled woodworker and now he is training Noah. Noah has his father's eye for wood.*

"I have taken to hiding items around the house for the others to find, but they are too accomplished as seekers. They require a bigger challenge. Now that they are asleep, I have time to stretch my imagination to compete with theirs.

"I must be clever enough to challenge Sarah, yet simple enough not to exclude Frederick. I have it!

*"Hunt around the house
and take a good look
for a very secret place
you might hide a book."*

"What do you think?" Aury asked, looking at her companions. "Any ideas?"

"You can hide a book anywhere," Carla mused.

"Where do we even start looking?" Suzanne asked.

"She said the kids were stuck inside. It would only make sense that the spot is somewhere in the house," Debbie said.

"And almost certainly not in the kids' rooms, since they were sleeping," Carla said.

"The library is the obvious choice," Pat said.

"Too obvious," Aury added.

"Read the clue again," Linda said.

Aury read it aloud.

"A secret place. Then not somewhere out in the open," Suzanne said.

"It's an old house. They might have had hidden compartments almost anywhere," Carla said.

"Do you think she hid a book, or that was just to give them an idea of the size of the space?" Pat asked.

"Good point," Aury said. "The first thing we thought of when we read about a book was the library. Maybe the compartment is somewhere in this room."

The ladies jumped to their feet and went to separate portions of the room. They knocked on walls and pried at every seam.

Debbie was dragging a chair across the floor to reach the higher shelves when Carla cried out from the archway between the library and the entry hall. "I found something."

The wall was extra thick to accommodate the fireplace that separated the rooms with ornate woodwork decorating the arch.

Carla pushed on the smallest of the carved squares. "I swear I heard it click."

"Do it again." Aury placed her hands on the wood.

This time when Carla pushed, Aury felt the wood shift, and she applied pressure to one side. The panel opened like a door.

The ladies let out a cry of delight.

"Way to go, Carla!" Pat said. "What's inside?"

Carla reached in and pulled out a wooden box about the size of a thick book. It was built from rough wood held together by tacks.

"Let's see the treasure," Debbie said.

Carla opened the box, pulling out a yellowed piece of paper. "It's another clue."

> *"Seek out the spot*
> *where the food is small.*
> *Expect lots of company.*
> *It is come one, come all."*

"I'll take the dining room," Aury said.

"I'll help you," Carla chimed in.

The rest of the women split off into pairs to search the house.

Aury started in one corner while Carla started in the other.

"Do you really think anything is hidden here?" Carla asked.

"I have no idea. But I can see how the hunt would keep kids

occupied." Aury got down on her knees and ran her hand along the baseboard, tugging anytime she thought she felt something loose.

"In here!" Linda called from the kitchen.

The ladies circled around Linda as she worked a broom handle to reach something behind the stove. They all waited in anticipation while she grunted and swore, trying to budge the stubborn obstacle.

She stumbled backward. "Finally!" Propping the broom beside the stove, she reached down and held up her prize.

"What is it?" Suzanne asked.

Pat started laughing. "Great job, Linda. You caught a mousetrap."

Linda dropped the box and brushed her hands on her pants.

"Not much of a prize," Carla said.

"I doubt that's what she hid for the kids," Aury said with a smile.

The women went back to their respective rooms to keep searching.

Daylight began to fade, prompting Pat to call a halt to their search. "I'm hungry. Let's see if we can make a meal out of what Scott and Aury scrounged up."

As the ladies finished their meal of baked beans heated in the fireplace and stale crackers, they went over the clues again.

"Maybe she wasn't referencing food," Linda said.

"What else could it be?" Aury stared out the window. The rain was coming down again. In the garden, she could make out a stone basin. Her eyes lit up as a thought came to her.

"I have an idea, but it'll have to wait until tomorrow. I'm tired."

Pat stayed seated as the others rose. "I'll watch the fire for a bit, then make sure it goes out completely before heading upstairs."

"Goodnight," Carla said.

The others echoed her, and they headed to their rooms.

Chapter 15

The next morning, Aury was up with the sound of birdsong.
"Girl, what are you doing?" Deb yelled from the doorway.

Aury raised her hand in a wave from her spot in the yard. "Pat, come help me with this," she called.

Pat slipped past Deb and walked toward Aury. "What's up?"

"Maybe she didn't mean people food. What about a bird feeder? Or a birdbath? Do you think that could be what this is about?"

Pat looked over the pitted and eroded gray statue. "Sure could have been. Looks like it was supposed to hold water."

"Help me tip it."

"She wouldn't have expected her kids to tip over a bird feeder," Pat reasoned.

"No, but it's shifted. Look at the rock it's sitting on."

Together they moved the waist-high birdbath over six inches.

"Doesn't that position make more sense?" Aury said, gesturing at the pattern in the stonework beneath the base.

"You're right. It fits better in that circle."

Aury picked up a stick and began poking around the stones making up the triangle pointing toward the house. "This one's loose," she cried out when the blueish-granite piece gave way.

Pat dropped to her knees beside Aury and helped her pry it up.

"What did you find?" Linda called from the house.

Aury reached in and pulled out a package wrapped in oilskin. She held it up triumphantly.

The ladies cheered. Aury and Pat got to their feet. With huge smiles, they joined the others in the dining room to unveil their prize.

Unwrapping the oilskin, Aury was surprised to find a small leather pouch.

"That's a strange treasure to hide for children," Deb said.

The ladies murmured agreement. Linda held the bag up to the light. "It might be a change purse."

"It has a clasp. See if you can open it," Pat said.

Linda used her fingernails to pry open the catch. A tiny piece of paper fluttered to the floor. Carla picked it up.

> *"Listen for toads*
> *With water in sight.*
> *Find the crag in the rock*
> *That catches the light."*

"Are you kidding me?" Deb said. "These kids would have lost interest by now and gone on to torture a cat or something."

Pat smacked her arm. "They had a better attention span than you do."

Linda studied the inside of the bag. "Do you think this is a picture?"

"Why would a change purse have a picture inside?" Carla asked.

"There's definitely something there." Linda passed the bag to Pat.

"We need a magnifying glass," she said.

"Well, let me just whip mine out of my bra," Deb said.

"You'd need a magnifying glass to see what's in your bra," Pat shot back.

"Does anyone have one in their sewing kit?" Aury asked.

"At the hotel," Carla offered. "I'm not sure which bag I shoved it into, though."

The ladies passed the leather pouch around, each guessing what it could be.

"It's too faded to make out," Suzanne said.

"Maybe it isn't a picture. Maybe it's just scratch marks from when it was made," Carla said.

"It could be a maker's seal," Linda suggested.

"I wonder why the pouch was still hidden? If the kids couldn't figure out the puzzle, you'd think Mary would have given them clues until they got it." Aury pulled out a chair and plopped down.

"They must have been interrupted," Linda said.

"Someone could have gotten sick," Carla said. "Sickness lasted a long time in those days, and they might have forgotten about the game."

"Good morning, ladies!" Scott's warm voice called from the doorway.

"In here," Aury called.

Scott entered the library bearing a tray of sandwiches and placed it on the coffee table. "The path is almost clear. You'll be able to make it home today," he said.

The ladies cheered at the news.

"We still can't get a car in here, so you'll have to walk most of the way. We have a cart waiting on the other side of where the road caved in to take you out to the road," Scott explained.

"No offense, Scott, but I'm looking forward to sleeping in my own bed again," Linda said.

"None taken. You've all been troopers, and I appreciate your patience."

"Aury has kept us busy with a treasure hunt," Carla said.

"Ah, yes, the treasure hunt. How's it going?"

"We've found three clues so far. This morning we found what we think was a change purse." Aury handed him the open pouch. She pointed to the mark on the inside.

Scott squinted at the picture. "What is it?"

"No idea. We thought you might know," Linda said.

He looked again. "It doesn't look like anything in particular."

"It came with a clue," Linda said. She read it to him.

Scott handed the bag to Aury. "You have your work cut out for you. Think you'll figure it out before dinner? I could use a buried treasure to rebuild this place."

"We'll do our best."

"I'll be back in a few hours to help the first two of you to the path."

"We'll be ready. Carla, I think you and Linda should go first. You have people waiting for you at home," Aury said.

"You'll get no argument from me," Carla said.

Aury followed Scott to the front of the house. "How bad is the damage?"

"Bad," he admitted. "I was barely making the payments before. I don't think I'll be able to recover from this."

"Won't the insurance help?"

"It will pay for some repairs, but with a storm this size, the insurance companies will be swamped. And I'll lose money from the other organizations I had booked to come in over the next six months." Scott forced a smile. "But there's a reason for everything."

"Maybe you'll be able to take the insurance money and build your new hall sooner than planned," Aury said.

"Good thought," Scott said. "Well, see you in a little while."

Aury watched him go, thinking how nice it would be to find a treasure for him.

Chapter 16

When Aury reentered the house, she found the ladies gathered in the dining room.

"Hey, Aury, want to join us? I found a deck of cards in my bedroom," Suzanne said.

"Not now. I think I'm going to head over to the motel while it's still light and see what we can save."

"I'll go with you," Pat said. "I need to get out of this house for a while."

"Should we all go?" Carla asked.

Aury thought about the trek through the woods and the debris that might block the path. "I don't think so. Let Pat and I check it out first, and we'll let you know what we find. Why don't you give us your car keys? We may be able to put some things into your cars if they aren't too wet."

"I left mine in my room," Linda said. "But my room's unlocked. I was in B-three."

Only Suzanne had her car keys with her, but the others told Pat and Aury where to find theirs. Fortunately, Carla thought she left her keys next to her sewing machine rather than in her room. Aury didn't think she would be able to unblock the door to Carla's room. She'd have to mention that to Scott. Maybe he could bring something for them to cut the brush.

Pat and Aury left the others to their card game and set off

through the woods. The ground was saturated from the deluge, and puddles dotted the path.

"It's a shame. It's pretty out here when the sun is shining," Pat said.

Aury agreed. "It's hard to believe there was such a big storm only a few days ago."

Fallen trees had blocked the path in several places. In some areas, they were able to climb over, but in others, they had to backtrack to find a way through the thicket. When they emerged into the clearing, their clothes were soaked through.

In the daylight, the damage to the motel looked worse than it had in the middle of the night. Many fallen trees had hit the building in addition to those that blocked safe passage for the vehicles.

Pat and Aury climbed through the broken window into the work area where the sewing machines were. The sour smell of wet cloth permeated the air. The majority of the damage was at the front of the room where a tree had punched a hole through the roof. Water dripped from various places in the ceiling where it must have traveled along the rafters to settle in low spots.

Sighing, Pat headed toward the kitchen area. "I'll grab some trash bags. Let's take what we think is worth saving. We can sort it out later."

Aury found one of the wagons they had used to haul boxes and equipment from the cars. She went from table to table, gathering sewing machines and quilting notions. Luckily, she knew where everyone had been sitting and was able to match their items to their cars.

Because both doors were blocked, they propped open a window at the front of the motel and passed things through the opening. It was slow at first, but they got into a rhythm. It took a few hours, but together Pat and Aury were able to clean out most of the workspace.

Suzanne's car was damaged, so they had to split her belongings into two other cars for eventual transport. Pat tied up the damp cloth in garbage bags.

"We'll need to wash this as soon as possible so it doesn't mildew. Some of it we can take to the house and lay it out to dry if you don't mind carrying things."

"Let's put some of the bigger pieces out on the cars. Then we won't have as much to haul," Aury suggested.

"Good call. I'm surprised so much of it stayed dry. We were lucky a tree didn't go through the roof."

They spread the largest pieces out on the hoods of the cars that weren't covered with debris. From the largest downed trees, they hung fabric over the branches. Aury stepped back and admired their work while Pat pulled a cell phone from her pocket and snapped a picture.

"This is one for the scrapbooks," she said.

Chapter 17

As promised, Scott returned, but it had been more than a few hours. This time he came bearing bags of cold cuts, bread, and cheese along with a cooler full of drinks. "Sorry for the delay. It took longer than we thought." He set the items on the kitchen table. "Grab some food, and we'll get going before it gets dark."

The ladies dug into the food.

"Aury, your grandmother called me back to check on you," Scott said.

That brought a smile to Aury's lips.

"She said she's sorry she missed this retreat, seeing as you are having so much fun without her."

"She must be feeling better," Aury said.

"I'm to tell you she's fine and staying where she is until they get the electricity situation sorted out. She's keeping the others entertained by teaching them games she played when she was younger."

Aury knew many of those games. Her grandmother had taught them to her when Aury stayed overnight. Gran didn't have a television set. She said it made for a lazy brain. Instead, she taught Aury logic puzzles and riddles.

"She would love the scavenger hunt," Aury said.

"We could use her help with some of these clues," Suzanne said.

"Maybe you can bring her out once we get everything cleaned up," Scott suggested.

Carla wiped her hands on a paper towel. "Okay, I'm ready. Let's get going."

"Do you need to get anything?" Scott asked.

Linda shook her head.

"Nope. Everything is at the motel, and the door to my room is blocked," Carla said.

"Oh, yeah," Aury said. "Do you think you could bring something to cut away some of the branches so we can get into the rooms?"

"I'll try on the next trip. You won't be able to haul all your stuff out, though, until we can get a vehicle out here. Is there anything you have to have?"

They all shook their heads.

"I'll still see what I can do. Alan's waiting for us. He's going to drive you to town," Scott said.

"Let's not do the next retreat during hurricane season," Linda said as she hugged Aury.

Aury laughed. "Where's your sense of adventure? Think about the story we'll have to tell when we talk about our quilts."

"See if you can find the treasure without us. *That* will be a great story," Carla said.

Aury walked with them as far as the hole in the road. The ground was still wet and extremely muddy in parts, so it took them over a half hour to reach the makeshift path around the hole.

Scott and Alan had cut the branches into the woods to the side of the trail. Alan helped Linda and Carla pick their way over hidden roots and underbrush. Once on the other side, they loaded into the four-wheel drive mini-Jeep waiting for them. It was open to the elements, but better than walking the last three miles to the road.

It was getting dark under the trees by the time they got settled. "I don't think we can make another trip tonight," Aury said.

Scott frowned. "I think you're right. I'm sorry. I thought we'd make better time."

"Don't worry about it. We can hang out for another night. Just bring more coffee in the morning?"

"Will do. Thanks for your patience," Scott said.

Aury waved before heading down the path toward the manor house.

Chapter 18

You're up bright and early," Pat said when she found Aury sitting in the kitchen the next morning.

"I kept thinking about our treasure hunt. After we found the first clue, we never went back to the diary. I thought since Mary Townsend put the first clue in there, maybe she wrote down the rest as well."

"And?"

"No such luck. Let me read you some passages.

I was right. Sarah got the first clue right away. When she puzzled out the second clue, I was pleased to see she did not speak the answer aloud. She waited and coaxed Frederick until he was able to discover the answer for himself.

"Then later she writes:

The weather has turned much for the better, but the children want to continue with the hunt. I stay up late at night designing new clues to keep them entertained.

Sarah has taken to uncovering the clues on her own but leaving them for Frederick to find in his own time. His young attention span does not match hers.

"That's the last time she mentions the treasure hunt. There's quite a bit more about the running of the household, how her garden fared through the storms, and her plans to make new clothes when James returns. But listen to this." Aury flipped through the diary until she found what she was looking for.

"February 15, 1862. James and Noah still have not returned. I am concerned as James does not typically leave for such a long stretch. Perhaps the weather early on delayed them."

She turned a few more pages.

"March 3, 1862. I have heard explosions in the distance. The sound carries across the river. We should be safe as we are far enough away that no one will chance upon us by accident. Since James has been gone with the horses, we have no way to plant the crops he planned. With no crops to take or destroy, we should avoid the interest of both sides of the fighting.

"We should at least take some precautions. I must prepare the children.

"There are a few more entries but then her diary ends quite abruptly," Aury said, closing the book and reclining in her seat.

"What is the date of the last entry?" Debbie asked.

"March 1862."

Pat opened a bottle of the room temperature water. "I wonder what she did to prepare the children."

"Or if they even made it through the war. Why would she stop writing?"

"Or leave her diary behind if she didn't have to?" Pat added.

The two were lost in their thoughts when Suzanne and Debbie joined them in the kitchen. Aury filled them in on what she had read.

"That makes the hunt a little less fun, thinking about what might have happened to the woman who made it up," said Debbie.

"Do you want to quit?" Suzanne asked her.

"Hell, no. There still might be hidden treasure, and I mean to find it." Debbie grabbed a package of crackers from their food stash in the middle of the table.

"Hello?"

"We're in here," Aury called.

Scott followed the sound of her voice into the kitchen. As promised, he carried a thermos of coffee and a paper sack of pastries.

The ladies ripped into the food unceremoniously. The coffee had lost some of its heat on its trip to the manor house, but it was fresh and comforting.

While they ate, Scott filled them in on the outside world. "Power is still out on this side of the river. Some people have generators." He gestured to the coffee. "But for the most part, the town is sleeping as businesses wait for their turn on the power repair list. This far out, you can imagine how low we are in the order of priority."

"What about Williamsburg? Have you heard anything?" Suzanne asked.

"The center of town has power again, but they're estimating five to six days before they can get to the neighborhoods. The hardware stores are giving away water by the case in their parking lots. The lines at the gas pumps are ridiculous because everyone wants gas for their generators."

"Not much to go home to," Pat said.

"But there's food in my pantry," Debbie said.

"You and your stomach. The two of you are very close," Pat said.

"That's because we have a lot in common!"

The others smiled.

"Who's ready to go home? I can take two more on this run and return for the last two," Scott said.

"I'll wait," offered Aury.

"Me too," Pat said.

Debbie grabbed another doughnut. "I'm ready. Let's go."

Suzanne and Debbie hugged the other two women. "We're counting on you to find the treasure," Suzanne said.

"We'll try not to disappoint," Pat answered.

When they had gone, Pat put the dirty coffee cups into the sink. "I hope they remember to wash this stuff when the power comes on or it's going to be nasty."

"I wonder how long this place has been boarded up?"

"They used to rent it out for weddings and events. My mom said she's been here." Pat ran her hand through the dust on the countertop.

"I would have liked to see it back then. Can't you imagine the dining room set for an elegant dinner?"

"Who would have thought you were such a romantic?" Pat brushed her hands together. "What do you want to do now?"

"Let's focus on our hunt. We're running out of time," Aury said.

Pat followed her into the dining room. She picked up the piece of paper while Aury went for the leather pouch.

"We should have grabbed a magnifying glass when we were at the motel," Pat said.

"Ta-da!" Aury pulled a small object from her pocket. "I'm sure Carla won't mind. I found it when we were packing the cars."

She took the small bag closer to the window and opened it wide for better lighting. She moved the glass until she found the right distance for the most clarity.

"I don't think it's a whole picture. I think it's part of something." She passed the glass to Pat.

Pat studied it. "I think it's a drawing, not a photo."

Aury took the glass again. Peering closely, her eyes squinted in concentration. "It looks so familiar. It's like having a word on the tip of your tongue but you can't think of it. Will you read the clue again?"

Pat read the poem aloud.

> *"Listen for toads*
> *With water in sight.*

Find the crag in the rock
That catches the light."

"Well, that's obviously the pond," Aury said.

"It sounds obvious, but Mary Townsend could be a tricky lady. It's a good place to start though."

They walked to the pond that separated the motel from the dining hall. It was still muddy because little grass remained along the path. The pelting rain had added a slick slime to the hard-packed dirt.

As they walked, they kept their eye on the pond, expecting to catch some glint of light.

"It has been almost two hundred years. What if the crag in the rock is gone?" Pat asked.

"Then we have spent a beautiful day enjoying a walk by the pond. No harm done."

"I wonder if the dining hall took any damage," Pat said.

Aury looked up at the stone structure where they had eaten their meals during the retreat. A tall tree was leaning, threatening to fall at the sign of a stiff breeze. "We should warn Scott to come cut that down before it has a chance to fall and cause more damage. That's the last thing he needs."

"It looks like that building's been here a long time. I'm surprised it hasn't taken a hit before now."

"I wonder what it was before. It's too far from the manor house to have been an outdoor kitchen," Aury observed.

"It could have been a stable. See how the roof's shaped? And where those double doors are, I bet that could have been a barn door."

Aury could see it as a barn. The peaked roof could have been a hayloft. "That's beautiful stone. I wonder what it is."

They strayed from their search by the pond to examine the dining hall more closely.

"I never paid much attention to the details in this building before. It's amazing how they could fit the pieces together so well."

"Crude, but effective," Pat said. "They weren't cut stone. They probably used whatever they could find."

"Check out the ironwork on that lantern." Aury pointed to the black lamp attached to the side of the rockface. "I wonder if it's original too."

"If it is, it's been upgraded. It's electric now." Pat pointed to the wires running up the outside of the rock.

Aury had a sudden thought. "But what if it were here in Mary's time? Or at least something in its place? They would have needed light for the stable. Why not on the outside against the rock that wouldn't catch fire?"

"I suppose. So?"

"The building's made of rock. What if this is the rock we should be looking for? Not down by the water?" Aury was excited. She ran her hands over the rough stone, starting at the base under the light and working her way up the wall. Pat caught on and started helping her.

"The clue says, 'catches the light.' What would catch the light?" Pat asked.

"Metal. Certain stones. A mirror."

"Water," Pat tossed out.

"We're too far away from the pond for it to reflect the light from a lamp here," Aury said.

"But if this was a stable, wouldn't there have been a water trough?"

Aury's eyes sparked. "Great idea." She backed up and looked at the ground in front of the dining hall. Pointing, she said, "There's a raised line of rocks parallel to the front wall. Do you think that could have been it?"

Pat went to where she was pointing. "It's the right shape."

"If there was a trough here, where could Mary Townsend have hidden a treasure?" Aury sat on the ground next to one end where the rocks were piled slightly higher than in the middle. She pushed and pulled on the stones, trying to move them. They didn't budge.

Pat sat on the opposite end and tried the same thing. "I give up. If there was something here, it must be gone by now."

Aury leaned on her hands, thinking. Her eye caught a gleam from the ceiling above the lamp.

Jumping to her feet, she got closer to the building. "I can't reach it," she said.

Pat looked around but the storm had blown everything away that might have been useful. She made a cradle of her hands and allowed Aury to put her foot in it for a boost.

Aury pushed on the shiny piece of metal and it gave slightly. Rust flaked down into her hair. She pushed it again, and the sheet slid out of its fasteners.

She placed her hand in the opening but nothing was there. "I'm sure this had to be what she was talking about. The metal was put there to reflect the light and make it brighter, like a mirror would." She stepped down, and Pat shook out her hands.

Aury walked to the other side of the door and inspected the ceiling. "Here's another one," she said.

"There might have been a light there too at one time," said Pat. She made another foothold for Aury.

"Your turn," Aury said, cradling her hands.

"No way. I'd hurt myself. You go. Just be quick."

Stepping up, Aury moved the metal sheet in one try. A larger hole appeared in the opening. She reached her hand around the inside edges and came out with a small container.

With both feet on the ground, she considered the cylindrical item. "My grandmother used to have tins like these. They were for storing teas, spices, and baking powder. Almost anything," Aury said. "Only hers had pictures on them. She used to collect them and display them above her kitchen cabinets."

"That one is rusted. Can you get the lid off?"

Aury struggled with it for a few minutes to no avail.

"Let me see it," Pat said. She took the tin and tapped it gently against the building. Rust flakes sprinkled the ground. This time, when she twisted the cap, it came off, leaving her hands with reddish-brown stains. She handed it to Aury and walked out to the grass to wipe her hands.

Aury tipped out the contents. She picked up the piece of paper first, anxious to read the next clue.

"Find the oldest variety
That from an acorn grew
Look under the roots
To find the next clue."

Pat picked up the remaining item, a two-inch by two-inch tile of wood. It was unfinished with bark still on one side. On the other was an indistinguishable pencil drawing. She held it out for Aury to inspect.

"It looks a lot like the first drawing," Pat said. "We need to use the magnifying glass again to be sure."

Aury smacked her hand against her forehead. "That's why the first drawing looked familiar."

"What?"

"Come here." Aury led Pat along the path then turned to face the dining hall. She held her arms out. "What do you see?"

"A building. I don't get it."

Aury pulled the leather pouch from her pocket. She turned it upside down and handed it along with the magnifying glass to Pat.

"It's a barn!" Pat cried. "She drew a picture of a barn."

"That's why it looked so close but not quite. The dining hall has changed a lot in one hundred and fifty years."

"And it's a crude drawing. She wasn't an artist or anything."

The talk of art reminded Aury of their quilts. "Oh, we need to get the fabric we hung in the trees before Scott comes to pick us up," Aury said, putting the trinkets inside the tin. "We'll have to resume the hunt later." She placed the tin in her pocket.

As Pat and Aury walked to the motel, Aury thought about how life must have been for Mary Townsend. No electricity, no indoor plumbing. The winters must have been brutal.

"Do you think you could survive in the 1800s?" Aury asked.

"Sure. Remember, it isn't like they were used to things one way and then lost them. They never knew any different. They must have been thrilled with every invention."

"We're spoiled. Think about washing clothes. We spend five minutes throwing clothes in the washing machine, then transfer them to the dryer. Can you imagine hauling clothes down to the river and spending hours with a washboard? Then hanging things to dry?"

"What about those downed trees? They'd have to clear them away with an ax and hand saws. Yep, no time travel for me. I think I'll rough it in current times with an occasional loss of power," Pat said.

Aury agreed. When they reached the motel, they pulled the fabric off the branches and folded it up. "That worked out well."

"At least it won't stink. We can stick it in my car, and I'll wash it when I'm home."

They loaded the fabric into Pat's trunk and headed to the manor house. Fewer puddles covered the path as the water had absorbed into the soil.

Chapter 19

Scott was sitting on the front porch when they got back. "I thought you gave up on me and decided to hike out on your own."

"Sorry," Aury said. "We had to finish packing stuff up at the motel."

"I didn't forget about tools to clear that brush. Everything's tied up trying to clear the primary paths."

"No worries. There's nothing we can't live without," Aury said.

Pat agreed. "Those sewing machines don't work without power anyway."

Aury pulled out the tin can. "We found our next clue." She showed him the piece of wood and the clue.

"There are so many trees around here, it would be hard to know where to start," Scott said.

"It must have been a unique tree—otherwise why would she think the kids could figure it out?" Pat said.

"Sorry, but I think you'll have to hold that thought for now. We better go, or Alan will wonder if we got lost," Scott said.

"Do you mind if I take these clues with me?" Aury asked. "I'll bring them back."

"You're welcome to them. I think it'll be fun to see what you figure out."

The walk to the hole in the road went quickly as Pat and

Aury filled Scott in on what they had found so far. When they cut through the woods to emerge on the other side where Alan waited, he greeted them with cold sodas and cookies.

"You're always feeding us," Pat said.

"It isn't a buffet, but it's better than stale crackers and whatever else you found to snack on," Alan said.

"We're quilters. We're used to snacking our way through the day at retreats. Quick energy boosts are all we need," Aury said.

"There's hot food waiting for you back in town. The diner set up grills and has been cooking up as much of their meat as they can. They're practically giving it away," Alan assured them.

As they bumped their way along the dirt road in the open maintenance cart, Aury felt a strange sadness about leaving. She took in the greenery, lush after the recent rains. Squirrels chased each other next to the path, and Aury laughed aloud when they noticed the vehicle looming over them.

She didn't remember taking the time to observe such things in her neighborhood. It was as if she were constantly in motion, repeating the same routine and not making headway.

Even with hot food awaiting her, she didn't relish giving up Eastover.

While Aury waited for her burger to come off the grill, she borrowed Alan's phone.

"Don't you worry about me," her grandmother assured her. "They're taking good care of us. They have a back-up generator, and we've been coping without a hitch. I was so worried about you, though. When the storm hit and I hadn't heard from you, I figured it was the power outage. When it had been over a day, I started to panic. Good thing your friend called when he did."

Aury smiled. When Gran started chatting, it was hard to get a word in. "I'm fine. I just desperately need a shower. And my car is still trapped at Eastover."

"Well, honey, you know where my keys are. Help yourself to whatever you need. Oh, the kitchen is going to be a mess. Don't go opening the fridge until you're ready to deal with the odor."

"Thanks, Gran. I'll have Alan drop me to pick up your car, then I'll come see you."

"Might want a change of clothes. I doubt they restored power at your place yet. You won't have any hot water."

"Good thinking. I'll do that. Do you need anything else?"

"Just to see your smiling face. I want to hear all about your adventures," Gran said.

"I'll be by in a few hours. See you then."

Aury disconnected and handed Alan his phone. "Thanks. I feel better now."

"Anyone else you want to call?" he asked.

"No. My parents died a few years ago in a car crash. No siblings, so it's just me and Gran now."

"Sorry to hear that. I'm sure she's glad to have you looking out for her."

"We look out for each other."

Alan smiled. "Let's fetch some food and get you home."

Chapter 20

A few hours later, freshly showered and dressed, Aury sat with her grandmother in the lounge of the hospital. The elder woman was much improved health-wise, but the doctors wouldn't release her until she had somewhere to go with power available. They didn't want her to relapse.

"And that's about it," Aury finished up with a recap of the quilting retreat. "They'll let us know when we can go out and collect our stuff."

"What a shame. That Scott fellow sounds like a nice young man."

Tilting her head, Aury lowered her chin and gave Gran a knowing look.

"What's that expression for?" Gran asked.

"No matchmaking. I'm not ready."

"Who said anything about matchmaking?"

"I hear it in your voice."

"Just because your ex was a snake doesn't mean all men are." Gran placed a reassuring hand on Aury's arm.

He was a snake, Aury thought. *But I wasn't much better.* She recalled the many fights they had because she married him expecting him to change. As if by her will alone, he would stop bar hopping and spend more time with her. She became the nag she always dreaded.

They didn't enjoy the same things, but she pushed and begged until he gave in and accompanied her on one adventure or another. It always ended in a fight, so she didn't know why she bothered.

"All I'm saying is I hate to imagine this Scott-fellow lose his family's dream." Gran's voice brought her back to the present.

"I know. I wish I could do something. I still have a few more days of vacation. I'm thinking about asking if he needs some help cleaning up."

"You were always handy with a chainsaw," her grandmother commented. "Scared all the boys away, I reckon."

Aury laughed. "It would be wonderful if we could solve the riddle and find some treasure for him."

Gran lounged in her chair. "Let's think about this.

Find the oldest variety
That from an acorn grew
Look under the roots
To find the next clue.

"You're right. It does sound like a tree. Pass me the piece of wood you found."

Aury dug it out of her bag and handed it to Gran.

"I'm not sure what kind of tree it could be. Maybe some type of oak. You could ask the Master Gardeners," Gran suggested.

"Who?"

"They're a club in town. Love to talk anything plant related. You'll see."

"I'll give them a call. I also want to find out if the library is open yet. They may have historical documents about Eastover."

"Good idea. Don't just focus on those computer files, either. Good libraries have the original records stored someplace," Gran said.

"There's a drawing on the other side."

Gran flipped the tile over. "It doesn't seem like much. Just some squiggles."

"That's what I thought, too. It could simply be scratches in the wood."

Holding it closer to her face, Gran squinted at it. "No, I would say more than scratches. But nothing I can make out."

"With all that happened, I can't say I wish you were there, but it was quite the experience. The manor house must have been beautiful in its day."

"I'm sure it was. Oh, and what a view of the river it must have. We'll have to go out there together once he gets it cleaned up."

"You would love the quilts we found. Handstitched and in great shape. They kept us warm throughout the storm when we had no heat," Aury said. "I should offer to have them cleaned for Scott. It's the least I can do. He won't want to store them after we used them."

"That would be lovely. Did they have labels on them?"

"I didn't even think to look," Aury said.

"The practice of affixing labels has been around a long time, so maybe whoever made the quilts labeled them, and if so, they should at least have a date and location. Possibly even the person they were made for and a message."

Gran smiled at a memory. "Your grandfather had labels made for me, embroidered with my name and lilacs because they were my favorite flower. Then all I had to do was add the other information."

"I have one of those on the quilt you made me. I didn't know Grandpa had them made for you. What a thoughtful gift."

"He knew how much time I spent on each one of those quilts and wanted to make sure people knew I was the creator."

Aury leaned over and squeezed her grandmother's hand. "I'll check the Eastover quilts when I go back. It'll be interesting to see how old they are. I hoped they're labeled."

"I think I'm going to lie down a bit," Gran said.

Aury stood and unlocked the wheels of the chair. "I'll give you a ride to your room."

"Why don't you take a drive around town and fill me in on how things look? I want to know how people are faring," Gran said.

"I can handle that." Aury guided the wheelchair through the hallway as her grandmother waved at various people, calling out to nurses and patients alike.

Having tucked Gran into her hospital bed, Aury followed her suggestion to go for a drive. Downed trees littered yards in the neighborhoods but had been cleared from the streets. Usually peaceful communities were humming in various pitches from multiple generators resourced to keep the basic necessities going.

Some houses had boards over windows while others displayed tape Xs used to discourage the glass from shattering in the storm. Aury assumed those folks hadn't returned from their evacuation yet.

Many of the principal streets appeared to have power restored, and the parking lots were full. Long lines snaked out of the gas station as people waited to purchase fuel for their generators.

Aury was pleased to find the library's lights were on. Parking spots were hard to find, and she had to drive several blocks away before she found street parking.

The library had more people than Aury had ever seen in there before. A sign next to the computer terminals let people know the internet was still down.

Luckily, Gran had mentioned there should also be paper records somewhere in the library. Aury approached the reference desk.

"Good afternoon. I'm looking for information about the Eastover Manor in Surry. Do you think you have anything about it?" she asked.

The librarian typed on his keyboard. "The internet's down, but we have our files on the network. They aren't as complete, and they're only for our records, but it's better than nothing."

The young man wrote something on a piece of paper and handed it to Aury. "Try here first. Let me know if you need more. These are in the basement."

"Thanks, I will." Aury read the coded letters and numbers and headed toward the stairs.

When she emerged at the bottom, the bright lights and cool air caught her off guard.

"What can I help you with?" an older gentleman asked.

Aury took in the wooden tables and library carts that were lined up at the front of the room. Rows upon rows of shelves reached out into the distance in front of her.

"I've never been down here before. I don't even think I knew the library had a basement."

The man smiled. "Most people don't. Some of the college kids have found it a quiet place to study—history majors or folks working on their advanced degrees. There's a lot to be said for secret places. What are you looking for today?"

Aury handed him the paper. "I'm interested in the Eastover Manor. Have you heard of it?"

"Heard of it! Why, I took my bride there for our honeymoon many moons ago." A smile lit his face. "The people were as nice as can be. The view out our window was one we talked about long after we left. Have you been out there? Is the house still standing?"

"I was there during the storm. The house is still there but it's in pretty bad shape."

"What a shame. I heard the woman who ran it got sick. Was it cancer? Can't remember. She sure was a spunky one." He got lost in his thoughts.

"That was probably Scott's mother. Scott Bell owns it now. He wants to get it fixed up. I was hoping to find some records of what it used to look like. I'm curious what else was on the property."

"I'm sure we have something that can help." The man led Aury between the stacks, stopping occasionally to check the note in his hand against the signs posted on the shelves. He finally came to a halt in front of a long set of metal drawers. Selecting one, he pulled it open to reveal file folders crammed with papers.

With practiced hands, he ran a finger along the top tabs until he found what he was looking for. He pulled out a thick folder and handed it to Aury. He reached in for another, then closed the drawer and led her into the open room.

"Make yourself comfortable" he said, setting the folder on one of the empty tables.

Hours later, Aury had pages of scribbled notes and a stack of photocopies the librarian had made for her of maps, deeds, and land plots.

"We're getting ready to close, young lady."

Aury looked up from the document she was reading.

"This is fascinating!" she said. "I never knew we had so much information down here."

"These days, if it's not on the computer, people aren't interested in digging. I find something satisfying about holding a piece of paper in my hand."

"I totally agree. Thanks for all your help with this." Aury gathered her things and put the papers into the folders.

"Always happy to help someone researching history."

"There's a whole library out at the manor house. Scott may be willing to donate some of the books. They're quite old."

The old man's eyes brightened. "That would be quite the treasure." He handed her a business card. "Will you pass this on to him for me? I'd be happy to come out and take a look. It would be nice to see the place again. Might even take my bride out for a picnic."

Aury smiled. "You might want to wait a while. The road is out leading up to the house, and many trees are down."

"Whenever he's ready," the librarian said.

Chapter 21

March 9, 1862

Mary Townsend sat in her favorite rocking chair on the wide front porch. She tried to concentrate on writing in her journal. She ran her hand lovingly over the cover. Her father had slipped it into her hands as she and James boarded the carriage for their trip south.

She thought she had glimpsed a tear on the old man's face, but it could have been the water in her own eyes as James prodded the horses.

A loud crack turned her head. It was so hard to focus with the bang of gunshots in the distance.

Not for the first time, she said a silent prayer for the safe return of her husband and her darling Noah. They had been gone much longer than they needed to be to simply pick up provisions. Mary tried not to think of the many scenarios which could have delayed their travels—most with unhappy endings.

She heard Sarah calling after the children in the rear of the house. Mary didn't know what she would do without Sarah. Living out here, Sarah had to grow up much faster than Mary would have liked. She would have preferred to teach Sarah how to paint and embroider. Instead, most of their learning time was filled with numbers and farming. Not that those skills wouldn't be useful, but Mary wished she could give her kids a little more luxury time.

Hearing an uproar, Mary set down her journal and hurried through the front hall to the back porch. The boys wrestled with fierce passion as Sarah watched, baby Emily on her hip, urging on one then the other.

Mary placed her hands on her hips, ready to put a stop to it. Instead, she slipped her hands into her apron and observed as the boys paced in a circle, looking for the right time to strike. They were dirty but smiling, engaging in harmless fun.

A loud boom sounded from the river, followed by a thunderous crack, pulling the children from their play as each head turned toward the fierce clatter.

"Come into the house now, children. Clean up for supper." Mary waved the kids inside, anxious to remove them from the fighting too close to home.

Chapter 22

Present Day

The next morning, Aury crawled out from under her favorite quilt—the one Gran had given her when she graduated college. The deep, rich blues were accented with brilliant, tiny, pink flowers. Aury had never been a pink-girl, but the bright spots of color on the dark fabric always brought a smile to her face.

The morning sun shone through the closed blinds, and the blank, lifeless face of the digital alarm clock stared at her as she stuffed her feet into slippers and pulled a sweatshirt over her head. She reached into the back of the closet, pulling out an old suitcase she rarely used. She had left her good one at Eastover.

She tossed some things in it she would need for a few days. There was no telling how long the power would be out.

Her stomach rumbled as she emptied the contents of her refrigerator into the trash bag. Thankfully, she didn't have much. Living alone, she tended to eat cereal for dinner many evenings.

She carried her suitcase in one hand and the trash bag in the other as she made her way to Gran's car. She pulled the trash can down to the road, knowing it may sit there for days before the company got on a regular schedule again.

Aury headed to the center of town, looking for an open restaurant. Oliver's was open, and she found a parking spot as someone left.

As she waited for her omelet, she pondered the clues. She was excited to share her findings with Scott, but first, she'd visit the Master Gardeners. She had found one of their flyers hanging on the library bulletin board and made an appointment to see the club's president; he might be able to help with the tree clue.

The waitress placed a steaming plate in front of Aury and rushed off to the next table. Apparently, a power outage in the residential areas was good for business in the center of town.

Aury ate promptly and paid her bill. A short walk brought her to the James City County office complex. She took the steps up to the third floor.

"Welcome! So glad you found us." Eleanor Parker was a spry, petite woman, but her smile was broad and her enthusiasm contagious. "Come in and have a seat." She waved at a gentleman sitting behind a computer screen. "Keith, this is the young lady who called with some questions about trees."

Keith started to stand.

"No, please. Don't get up for me. Thank you for taking the time to see me," Aury said. She leaned over the desk and shook his hand.

"What can we help with?" Eleanor asked.

"Well, first I'd like to read you something. It's a riddle I'm trying to solve." She read the clue out loud.

> *"Find the oldest variety*
> *That from an acorn grew*
> *Look under the roots*
> *To find the next clue."*

"I feel a little silly," Aury admitted.

"Don't," Keith said, smiling. "You will be looking for an oak tree, but there are over ninety species of oaks. Seeds from some other trees are called gumballs, horse chestnuts, pinecones, you get the idea."

Aury gave him an astonished look. "How did you know what I was going to ask?"

"It's a common question, actually. Most people could tell you a tree grows from an acorn, but they don't always know what kind of tree," Keith said.

"People see an acorn and think of two things: squirrels and trees," Eleanor said.

"Another fun fact most people don't usually know is squirrels can be picky eaters. They'd rather eat acorns from the white oak group when they find them and store the red oak acorns for later."

"The red oak acorns have tannin, which is bitter-tasting, so the squirrels put off eating those until they have to," Eleanor added.

Aury smiled. "So what's the oldest variety of oak here in Virginia?"

"Depends where in Virginia. Most likely something from the white oak group. The Southern live oak—*Quercus virginiana*—lives a long time," Eleanor said.

"That's the tree most often associated with Virginia and the south. You ever see those old movies with the huge trees covered in draping moss? Those are Southern live oaks," Keith said.

Eleanor pulled a book off a shelf and started flipping through the pages. When she found what she was looking for, she handed the book to Aury. "Look at those roots. They're hardy trees, able to grow in salty soil so they do well around the coast."

Aury studied the picture, trying to envision a tree like that on the property somewhere. Then she remembered something she read in the archives the day prior.

She stood and handed the book back to Eleanor. "Thank you both for all the help."

"We didn't do much. If you have any more questions, stop by and see us," Eleanor said.

Keith gave a friendly wave as Aury departed.

Chapter 23

March 21, 1862

Sarah presented the bag of eggs to her mother. "Not as many today as usual," she said.

"It's fine. We need to give them a little more feed." Mary ran her hand down the top of her daughter's blonde locks to her shoulder. *She'll make a wonderful mother and wife if we ever get through these battles,* she thought.

"Is Daddy coming home today?" Sarah asked.

"I pray so." Mary couldn't think of a better response. False promises were not her way. "Get the boys moving on their chores, please."

Sarah lightly kissed her mother's cheek and left to do as she was told.

Emily tottered over to her mother and hung onto her skirt. Mary swept her into her arms and spun her in a circle.

"You are a blessing, little one. Do not ever forget it."

Emily smiled and pulled at the rose-engraved locket Mary always wore around her neck.

"Shall we make breakfast? Perhaps grits this morning with leftover bread from last night's supper." Mary busied herself in the kitchen, chatting all the while with Emily.

"When Daddy comes home, maybe we can take a carriage

ride. Would you like that?"

She opened the pantry door, disappointed to discover she was down to her last bag of flour. She sighed as she pushed the bag aside and reached for the remaining cornmeal. "We'll just eat more oats. The horses aren't here to feed anyway."

The boys entered the kitchen like a whirlwind, poking and punching each other.

"Now, now," Mary scolded. "Did you finish weeding the garden?"

"Yes, ma'am," Frederick and Thomas said in unison, straightening up to address their mother.

"How does it look?"

"The plants are showing green tops," Frederick answered. "But the rabbits have started eating them before we have a chance to."

"Can we pull up the radishes?" Thomas asked.

Mary smiled. "Not yet. I'll let you know when. Go wash up. We'll eat soon."

The boys scampered off.

"We need to put up a better fence. One more thing to add to the list, little Emily. Are you going to help?"

Emily giggled and clapped her hands.

"Yes, I think this is going to be a chore we can all share."

Chapter 24

Present Day

W"ait until you see what I found!" Aury told Scott as she jumped out of her grandmother's car. They stood on the dirt road halfway to where the road had collapsed. Bits of tree bark and sawdust covered the mud patches, giving them a quicksand-like appearance. Logs surrounded him in a pattern of disarray.

His jeans were caked with mud, and his wet shirt was plastered to his chest. He set aside the chain saw he was carrying and wiped his hands on a rag from his pocket.

"You look refreshed," he said.

Aury stopped, suddenly self-conscious. "I'm sorry. I wasn't thinking. Do you have a place to stay with electricity?"

A broad grin spread across his face. "I'm fine, really. I think of it as an extended camping trip. We used to camp a lot when I was young. What did you find?"

She pulled a notebook from the canvas bag flung over her shoulder. "The library had information about this area going back to the sixteen-hundreds.

"According to Mary's diary, the Townsend family moved here in 1846. Check out these maps I found."

Aury started to unfold a sizeable piece of paper she had

tucked into her notebook.

Scott laid a hand on her wrist. "Why don't we go find a place to sit and discuss this? I'm ready for a break." Scott picked up his saw and led the way to a cart waiting nearby.

As they bounced their way around the fallen trees and debris, Scott quizzed Aury on the conditions in Williamsburg.

"It's not near as bad as here. Of course, most of the residential areas don't have power, but the center of town does. They've brought in power companies from Maryland, New York, and Pennsylvania. They're working around the clock."

"That's good to hear. The folks out this way have been helpful. A few started clearing fallen trees without me having to ask. I miss that neighborly comradery living in the city."

They pulled up in front of one of the cabins Aury and Scott had scavenged during the ladies' stay in the manor house. A picnic table had been set up outside the main door next to a small fire circle built from stone. Twenty feet around the area had been raked.

"Have a seat," Scott offered. "I'm going to wash up." He walked behind the cabin. A moment later, Aury heard the creaking of an old-fashioned hand pump on a well, followed by the sound of gushing water. It reminded her of the days she had spent visiting Girl Scout camps in her youth.

While she waited, she picked up rocks to weigh down the corners of the various maps. She laid one out on the table.

"What's so exciting?" Scott asked.

Aury pointed at a map as she told him what she had discovered. "These maps are from different years. You can tell as the details get better and better." Her finger traced the line of the James River.

"Here's the river. This is where Eastover sits." She noted a spot on the map. "And look here." She put her finger on a spot where the land jutted into the river slightly. *Tree Point* was neatly scripted. She showed him an older map. "Here they only have an x in that spot. And going back further," she switched maps again, "that same spot is always marked somehow."

"It must have been a big tree to make its way onto a map as a marker," Scott said.

"Do you think you could find that spot now?"

"I think so. But I don't remember a huge tree."

"It may not be there anymore."

"Let's go on a treasure hunt," Scott said. He took a shovel from a nearby wheelbarrow while Aury folded up the maps and stowed them in her bag. She held one in her hand to help guide them.

They climbed into the cart and headed toward the river.

Before they reached their destination, Scott slowed the cart to a stop. "We have to walk from here; it's too overgrown to drive."

Aury gazed at the line of bushes and trees. Even though the chance of the tree still standing was remote, she felt a pang of disappointment that no one tree towered above the rest.

Moving through the tree line, Aury imagined how it would have appeared in 1861. They reached the edge of the cliff overlooking the river, and Scott took in a deep breath of moist air.

"Let me see the map again."

They oriented themselves with the bends of the river, then Scott headed off to the north. One hundred yards away, he stopped again. "It should be right around here."

Aury began a methodical search of the ground, starting at the cliff edge and working her way deeper into the trees. "Here!"

Scott left off his search to join her. Aury stood above him on a platform the size of a small stage. She had pulled away ivy and weeds to reveal the stump of a tree. "This has got to be it!"

He circled the stump. "Now what?"

"We should have brought two shovels," Aury said.

"I've got it." Scott rammed the shovel into the dirt at the base on the side furthest from the water.

"This tree had to be large even in 1861. Would Mary have made the children dig all around it to find the clue?" Scott asked.

"They would have seen fresh digging marks, so they

wouldn't have to search very hard."

"But they were kids. Would they apply that kind of logic?"

Aury jumped off the stump to examine the bark more closely. After a few minutes on her hands and knees, Aury said, "Does this seem like a natural mark to you?"

Scott jammed the shovel into the growing pile of dirt and walked to where Aury was pointing. The line in the bark was perpendicular to the ground and darker than the area surrounding it. A shorter line cut across the top to form a cross. It was shallow and would have easily been unnoticed if they weren't hunting for it.

"The lines are too straight to be natural," Scott confirmed. He grabbed his shovel and started digging at the base of the cross.

"What do you think it is?" Aury asked when Scott's shovel thudded at the bottom of the hole.

"Another clue." Scott grunted as he scooped the dirt from the hole. He pulled out a tin box, corroded with only faint signs that there had once been a design. He tapped it against the shovel head to break off some of the rust and handed it to Aury.

Sitting down on the stump, Aury pried the lid off the ten-inch square box.

The paper was brown and thin. Holes appeared along the creases where it had been folded for so long. She read it aloud.

"Stay on dry land
With water under your feet.
As we carefully planned
Stay out of the heat."

"How many clues did this lady leave for her kids?" Scott said as he filled the hole.

Aury shrugged. "Guess we need to keep searching. What do you think about this clue?"

"Dry land with water under your feet sounds like a bridge."

"You're right. Do you have any bridges on your property?"

"Not anymore. I don't know why they would have needed

one in the 1800s either. We have a few streams, but you can step over them."

"Stay out of the heat," Aury mused aloud. "Think that means in the shade of the trees?"

"There are so many trees on this property, that doesn't help to narrow things down. I think we need to let this one simmer for a while. In the meantime, I have some things to get done."

"What can I do to help?"

Scott grinned at her. "You'll be sorry you asked."

They climbed into the cart, heading to the fallen debris and Scott's chainsaw.

After picking up work gloves for Aury, they proceeded to clear the path. Scott cut away limbs and branches, and Aury dragged them off the road into a pile for burning later.

They worked in companionable silence, interrupted only by the buzz of the saw.

With their task completed, Scott loaded the tools into the cart. "Thanks for your help. That went much faster with two people."

"Of course. I wish I could do more."

"The Army Corps of Engineers are coming to inspect the hole in the road tomorrow. They're going to assess the damage and let me know if I need to repair it or find another way in."

"The Corps? How did you rate so high?" Aury asked.

"A friend of mine works for them. They're coming out to inspect the power lines in this area, and I told him we have some vehicles blocked out here. They may be able to put up a temporary bridge so we can get equipment in and your cars out."

"I thought they only did things for the military."

"Nope." Scott started the bumpy drive to the cabin. "During emergencies, they work for FEMA."

"Hey, I mentioned the Eastover library to the archivist, and he's excited to see some of your old books. Hope you don't mind," Aury said.

"Not at all. He's welcome to them. I can't imagine there's anything that interesting," Scott said.

"You would've never imagined a treasure hidden on your property either."

"We aren't sure there actually *is* a treasure. Don't get your hopes up."

Aury smiled. "Too late. Do you mind if I take a few books for him to scan through?"

"Help yourself. They aren't doing anyone any good here."

Aury entered the cool, musty interior of the manor house. Before going to the library, she went upstairs to check the labels on the quilts—Gran was right. Each was labeled; one was dated 1846 as a wedding gift to Mary and James. Flipping over the corners of each, she took snapshots with her phone.

She made a mental note to talk to Scott about washing these since the ladies had used them during their stay. Her grandmother would know if they needed special care.

She went to the library and took her time running her hand along the book spines. She selected a few titles and added them to the growing pile. She felt she had a decent sampling to take to the library. It might be a while before the archivist could make it out here himself.

Her eye stopped on the title *The Children of the New Forest*. As she tried to take it from the shelf, it stuck to the book next to it. She gently tugged until it pulled free.

The edges of the book were dented and the board under the cover showed through in places. It was obviously well-loved. Gently opening it, she saw scrawled in curly penmanship, "To my darling Frederick. I hope you enjoy this book as much as I have. Love, Mother."

Retreating to the nearby sofa, Aury instantly got lost in the story about the four orphaned children being raised as the grandchildren of a forester. Just as they were about to rescue the gypsy boy Pablo, Aury turned the page to find a piece of loose, yellowing paper tucked into the book.

"You about ready to go? It's getting dark," Scott said from the doorway.

Startled, Aury looked up. "Sorry, I got sidetracked by this

old book." She tilted it to show Scott the colorful, although somewhat faded, cover. "Mary gave it to one of her sons. I found another note inside."

Scott came closer to peer over her shoulder.

Aury unfolded the paper. "The handwriting is different on this one."

> *F,*
>
> *I had to put things away, but only you, Mother, and I will know where. It is crucial to keep Father's papers and Mother's special gifts away from anyone stopping at Eastover. We do not know which side they will be on. Better not to take chances.*
>
> *Leave them hidden until all is safe. Then keep going with Mother's game.*
>
> *If I am not here, you have to take care of the little ones. Mother needs us to be strong.*
>
> *S*

"S? Could that be the oldest daughter?" Aury asked.

"Makes sense. Who else would know the secret hiding places?" Scott said.

"What happened to their mother? Why couldn't she care for the kids?"

"I don't know. Was it in the diaries you found?"

"No. They just ended in March 1862. I'll go to the library and see if I can find out what could have interrupted Mary's writing."

Chapter 25

April 11, 1862

B ut why do you have to go?" Thomas whined.

"Many people are getting hurt. Someone needs to take care of them," Mary answered gently. Sitting in the safety of their cozy parlor, it seemed unreal that people were dying across the river.

"But who will take care of us?"

"Sarah will watch after you."

"I'll do it," Frederick argued. "I'm the man of the house. Papa said so when he left."

"You can do it together," Mary said to him. "I won't be gone long. Just a few days at a time. I'll come home often and bring you news." *And food.* She didn't want to voice her concern over the lack of supplies.

The news brought by the rider from the Army of the Potomac was just in time. They were looking for women to help the soldiers in the hospitals. The army would pay in food for the assistance rendered.

Mary could tend the wounded. She had never been squeamish around blood, even when Noah had put a nail through his foot while working on the barn.

She could write letters for the men who couldn't write

themselves. Overall, she would be helping the injured and helping her family at the same time. Part of her hoped to get word about James and Noah, but she was also afraid of what she might discover.

"You have chores to do, and Sarah will continue with your lessons."

The boys groaned while Emily clapped her pudgy hands.

"I'm going to be a soldier. I don't need to learn my letters," Frederick declared.

"Then I don't either," Thomas added.

Mary sighed. *Why do little boys think war is glamourous?* "Your father is going to expect you to be ready to help him with the books when he gets home. You don't want to disappoint him."

Thomas threw himself against the sofa cushions, his arms across his scrawny chest.

Sarah was trying to be brave, but Mary saw the wetness in her eyes threatening to spill over. "We will be fine, Mother. Do not worry about us. How will you get to town?"

"The soldiers are sending a wagon for me, along with other women in the area. They will pick us up at the church building in the morning and drop us off there in a few days. They will keep this rotation going for as long as needed."

"You won't sleep here?" Thomas asked, on the verge of tears.

"I will sometimes. It will be easier if I stay in town a few nights rather than spend so much time on the road traveling back and forth. I need you all to be brave while I'm gone."

"It will be an adventure," Sarah said. "We will pretend we are grown, and this is our homestead to keep."

"It is ours," Thomas said.

"Yes," Sarah agreed. "But now we make the decisions without having a mother telling us what to do." Sarah winked at Mary.

Mary smiled at the courage Sarah was showing. She would

get her siblings through this stage of their lives. Mary just hoped it would end soon enough to allow Sarah the chance to play without the heavy burden on her shoulders now.

"Get changed for bed. Go now. There will be time for a story before we put out the light. What do you want to hear?" Mary asked.

"The children in the forest!" Frederick said before the others even had a chance to think about their choice.

Mary laughed. "Fine. We'll read *The Children of the New Forest*. Go wash. I'll tuck you in."

As Sarah picked up Emily and ushered the boys to the stairs ahead of her, Mary stood and ran her hand along the books on the shelf. She loved when her mother read to her. Even now, she could imagine her mother's arms wrapped around her as they snuggled together for a story.

Books were a luxury, but Mary's father was a firm believer in education for girls as well as boys. He was an astute businessman who knew where to invest his money. His textile factory in Philadelphia, Pennsylvania, was doing a good trade. Mary never wanted for anything—books especially.

She wanted to give her kids the same luxuries but living on a farm in Surry County was not turning out to be what she expected. She didn't mind the labor. She enjoyed tending the soil and toiling beside her husband on various projects. While he felled the trees in the forest, she kept the books and prepared the invoices for payments.

Now she would have to pass the bookkeeping chores to Sarah along with the keeping of the house. With no one to continue the logging work, only household records would be required. She would have to give Sarah a journal of her own to keep track of these trying times.

Chapter 26

Present Day

As Aury scribbled furiously in her notebook, her elbow hit the stack of books next to her, toppling them to the floor. Multiple heads whipped up to stare at her as she whispered her apologies in the quiet of the library.

History was never her strong suit, but she was fascinated by what had taken place in this very town. She knew Colonial Williamsburg as a tourist attraction and had walked through the museums at Jamestown and Yorktown, but those excursions only impacted her on a surface level.

With Mary's diary, Aury now felt connected to the past in a way she never had before. She felt as if she was reliving history through a friend's eyes.

In her furor to figure out what actions had made Sarah hide the family treasures—whatever those might be—Aury pulled maps and old letters from the archives.

Once again, she'd become so immersed in her research, she was surprised to hear the librarian announce closing time. Aury reluctantly packed up what she had been working on and returned some of the books to the area to be reshelved. The others, she took to the checkout desk.

Gran put the last of her belongings into the waiting suitcase and zipped the top closed. "Let's get going. I need to see what kind of shape my house is in after so many days away."

Aury picked the suitcase up off the bed. "The electricity came on yesterday. The neighborhood is getting back to normal. And it's not as noisy now that the generators have been switched off."

"I should get one of those," Gran commented. "Would've saved the food in my fridge."

"You didn't have that much. I threw it all away already."

"Thank you, child." Gran put her arm around Aury's waist as they walked down the hall and out of the rehabilitation hospital.

"We found the next clue," Aury said, as she slid into the driver's seat.

"You did? Where?"

Aury told her about digging up the tin at the base of the tree. "But now we're stumped again."

Gran gave her a sideways look. "That was a really bad pun."

Aury laughed. "Sorry, it wasn't supposed to be a pun."

"So give me the clue."

They pulled into the restaurant parking lot where they had reservations for dinner. "You'll have to wait until we get inside. I don't have it memorized."

After they were seated and had placed their order, Aury pulled out her notes and read the poem.

> *"Stay on dry land*
> *With water under your feet.*
> *As we carefully planned*
> *Stay out of the heat.*

"We think the dry land over water could be a bridge and out of the heat could mean in the shade," Aury said.

"Could be. But sounds too straightforward for your writer. She seems to be a little trickier than that." Gran rolled the stem of her water glass between her fingers as she thought. "What did you find at the library?"

Aury turned the page. "As part of the Army of the Potomac, the chief engineer Brigadier General AA Humphreys was sent to do a reconnaissance of the area so the Union troops could take Richmond from the east in 1862."

She went on. "Mary's diary says they heard gunshots and got scared. That would make sense. The Battle of Williamsburg was raging across the James River. Sound carries over water." Aury handed her grandmother a map and pointed to the spot where Eastover was located.

"What does this have to do with the puzzle?" Gran asked.

"What if James and Noah got caught up in the fighting? That's why they didn't come back."

Gran nodded along with Aury's enthusiastic musings.

Aury glanced at her notes again. "The Confederate force, known as the Army of the Peninsula, led by General John Magruder, created ruses to fool invaders as to the size and strength of their forces. It slowed them down. What if they came up the James River? Mary or Sarah could have been scared enough to hide their valuables."

A waiter placed their meals in front of them. "Eat your food before it gets cold," Gran said.

Aury shoveled a bite into her mouth but kept talking. "The Civil War was heating up then. In the spring of 1862, the Peninsula Campaign saw a lot of fighting as the Union troops tried to take Richmond from the east. Surry would have been a natural place to stop and regroup. What if they did something to Mary? That would explain why she stopped writing in her diary."

"You could be right. It was a brutal time."

"Where would I find information about Mary and her family?"

"Churches keep birth and death records. If they were buried

nearby, you could check headstones," Gran suggested.

"That's brilliant!" Aury jumped to her feet.

Gran gestured sternly at the chair. "Sit down, young lady. They've been dead this long. They aren't going anywhere."

Aury sat, replacing the napkin in her lap. She could barely contain her excitement as she finished her dinner.

Chapter 27

April 24, 1862

Mary was exhausted as she rested on her haunches to relieve her back. The hospital floors were in constant need of scrubbing, and all the women took shifts to keep them clean. She would be glad when this week was over, and she could return to Eastover and her children.

She thought of them constantly. Sarah would run a fine household someday, and even Frederick was taking his part as the man of the house seriously. He and Thomas had constructed a fence of sorts to keep the rabbits out of the garden. It leaned a bit where they couldn't sink the posts deep enough, but it held.

The extra food Mary was able to take home extended their stores. While she was getting thinner, the kids appeared to have grown each time she returned home. Frederick's pants were too short now; she made a mental note to check the general store for material. She could always write to her father but wasn't quite ready to fill him in on their situation yet. She was sure his textile mills were busy producing uniforms for the Union soldiers.

Besides, getting a letter through the Confederate forces to the north may be too difficult under the present circumstances.

The hospital matron walked by, pulling Mary out of her

reverie and to the task at hand. She leaned into her work, anxious to finish before supper rounds.

Chapter 28

Present Day

Aury pored over the old maps, searching for a bridge symbol. Scott was right; there were no markings for rivers or streams on the property. The nearest water source was the James River, and they hadn't built a bridge over it until early 1900s.

Standing, she stretched, then bent at the waist like she made the quilters do. Sitting in one spot too long wasn't good for her body or mind. As she twisted and turned to release tense muscles, she marveled over how quickly things can change.

Three days ago, her biggest concern was which random pieces of fabric looked best together. Now she was following a century-old treasure hunt. While she loved seeing the final composition when a quilt came together, this quest was more exciting because she had no idea how it would end.

Glancing at her watch, Aury decided she had time for a walk to clear her head.

The sounds of buzzing chainsaws replaced the usual chirping of birds in her neighborhood. It was good to see things returning to normal. The electricity was on in most developments, and city trucks had been driving around picking up debris.

After spending so much time at Eastover, the houses on half-acre lots made her feel claustrophobic. She already missed the smell of the river and the physical labor that came with the outdoors.

How else would you stay out of the heat? Her mind kept reverting to the puzzle. They didn't have air conditioning or electric fans. Staying in shaded areas was the only thing she could think of.

A horn honked, causing her to jump. She looked over her shoulder to see Gran behind the wheel, a smile on her face.

Aury waited until she pulled alongside and rolled down the window.

"You scared me half to death," Aury said.

"You were daydreaming and not paying attention to your surroundings. Get in and tell me where your mind was."

Aury got into the car, and Gran drove toward Aury's house.

"I've been thinking about your clue," Gran said. "If you were trying to stay out of the heat, where would you go?"

"Somewhere out of the sun where there's a breeze."

"Eastover is on the James River, right?"

"Right. The manor house sits on a cliff above the water."

"Water is cool. What if she is pointing them toward the water?"

"But the clue says stay on dry land."

"If we rule out the dry land being a bridge, what else has water running under your feet?"

"You got me," Aury said.

"Before refrigeration, the only way to keep food cool was in a springhouse. In the eighteen-hundreds, they built sheds near the river. A trench of river water flowed through the dirt floor of the springhouse, keeping the room cool year 'round. Old-fashioned refrigeration of sorts."

Aury looked at her grandmother in awed appreciation. "That's amazing. How did you think of that?"

"I was thinking about all the food you had to throw away when the electricity went out. Then I remembered my grandmother setting a bucket of our picnic food in the river to keep it cool when we were going to be out all day." Gran pulled into the driveway.

"It fits." Aury was excited as she hopped out of the car. "You would plan to build a springhouse. I wonder if it is on any of the maps."

Gran followed her into the house, and Aury sorted through the papers on her kitchen table until she found what she was looking for.

Running a finger along the river, she found a small square on the map.

"What do you think? Could this be it?" she asked Gran.

Gran squinted at the paper. "Show me where the main house was."

Aury indicated a larger rectangle only inches away.

"Is the building on the river still there?"

"I don't remember seeing it, but we can ask Scott." Aury placed the call.

He answered on the fourth ring. Aury filled him in on their speculations.

"There's no building along the river that I know of. I've walked that beach many times, and I think I would have remembered."

"When will you be at Eastover again?" Aury asked him.

"I'm already here. I took a few more days off because I have to meet with some contractors.

"Do you have time for more treasure hunting?"

She heard him chuckle at his end of the line. "Who could resist a treasure hunt?"

Chapter 29

Scott followed the squiggle of the river on the map, matching it with the landscape in front of him. "Over that way is where we found the tree," he said, as he gestured to the right, shovel in hand. "So we still need to move off more in that direction."

As they rounded the bend, Aury saw the cascade of vines she'd encountered on her first walk, prior to the storm. "Doesn't it seem unnatural in the way it grew?"

Scott used his shovel to poke through the mess of kudzu. "It's not rock or tree behind it. Too soft."

"Dirt?"

"No." He plunged the shovel in, and it stuck. This time he twisted. They heard a cracking sound.

"Wood?" Aury asked.

"I think so." He used the shovel blade like a scythe, pushing and pulling the kudzu apart.

Aury put on her gloves and tugged at the loosened weeds. Eventually, they made out the dim outline of steps.

"That makes sense!" Aury backed up to get a wider view. "The house sits on the top of this cliff. They'd need an easy way to get to the springhouse."

"Wooden steps built in the 1860s wouldn't still be here," Scott said.

"Not the original steps, but they may have been replaced

over time."

He pulled out the map again, trying to place the exact location of the square on the beach. "It should be around here." He gestured with open arms.

Aury slipped headphones over her ears.

"Tell me again how you happened to have a metal detector laying around your house?" Scott was amused.

She pulled the headphones down. "It was a gift from Gran when I was in high school. I told you she liked the idea of finding treasure. Williamsburg is filled with stuff buried in the woods from the many battles fought in this area. We searched for old bullets."

"Did you ever find any?"

"Please. I have the largest bottle cap collection this side of the Mississippi. If Mary hid the next clue in a tin, this should pick up on it." She put the headphones in place and switched on the device. Sweeping back and forth in front of her, she walked the area from the foot of the steps toward the water.

"Here!" she called out.

Scott dug where she directed. Seconds later, he reached down and picked something up. "Another cap for your collection." He tossed it at her.

She caught it and placed it in her pocket with a grin, then continued her sweeping motion. This time when she stopped, she held her excitement.

Again, the hole wasn't very deep when Scott unearthed a tin can. They repeated the process.

At the fourth hole, Scott came to an abrupt halt. "Aury, I think we need to stop."

"Why? Are you tired already? I can dig for a while."

He pulled the shovel out of her reach.

"What?"

"Aury, look." Scott signaled to where he had been working. Several small, tan, stick-like bones showed through the dirt he had overturned.

She leaned in to get a closer look. "Are those fingers?"

"Could be. Or they could be something from a small animal. I just think we need to have it checked out before we keep digging."

"We'll have to ride out to the road to get a signal," Aury said, still peering into the hole.

"Should we cover them up?"

"Probably. We don't want an animal to drag them off. Do you have a tarp or anything?"

"I didn't bring one. Let's just put the dirt back." Scott gently scooped up the dirt and replaced it in the hole.

Aury pushed more of the pile on top and lightly pressed it down. "Feels kind of sacrilegious to leave it here."

"It would be worse to leave the bones lying around."

"What if they're human?" Aury shuddered. "You have a dead body on your property."

Scott laughed at her. "I think you'd be surprised at how many properties have someone buried on them."

"Yes, but I don't know about them so it doesn't creep me out."

"Look on the bright side; it's not a fresh body."

She rolled her eyes. "Let's go. I want to find out who this is."

Scott placed both shovels in the cart, and they rode to where the road had caved in. They were relieved to see workers with "U.S. Army Corps of Engineers" stenciled on their work vests.

"Glad to see you," Scott said, extending a hand. "I'm Scott Bell. Thanks for taking care of this."

"No problem. I'm Frank and this is Barry. We're checking the area around the hole to see how big a temporary bridge needs to be to span it safely."

"Well, hopefully you have the right size bridge handy. I have a feeling we are going to get a lot of use out of it." Scott gestured to Aury. "This is Aury St. Clair. She's helping me with some work out here."

"You'll never believe what we found! Old bones!" she told them.

"Are you kidding?" Barry said. "Were they uprooted during the storm?"

"No, we were digging and came across them," Scott explained.

"We should call the police," Aury said.

"We have radio links set up. Hold on a minute." Frank pulled the small brick off his belt and pressed the button.

"This is Frank at Eastover. Can you send a patrolman up here to talk to the owner?"

A beep sounded when he released the talk button. Seconds later, a crackling voice answered. "What's the problem?"

"Owner found some old bones on the property." Again the beep.

"Roger. I'll make the call."

"Thanks," Scott said. "That will save us a trip into town."

"We're about done here," Frank said. "We'll head to the office and see if we can't put a priority on your bridge."

"Appreciate it. We'll wait by the cabin."

Scott and Aury rode silently to the picnic table. Scott went inside the cabin, then emerged with two bottles of cold water, dripping from the melted ice of the cooler. He handed one to Aury.

"Thanks." Aury held the cool bottle to her forehead. "It could be an old grave, I suppose."

"Wouldn't there have been some type of marker if it was a grave?"

"If the marker was made from wood, it would be gone by now."

They lapsed into their own thoughts again.

"We still don't know what happened to them . . . Mary's family, that is," Aury said. "Sarah left her brother a note in his book because she was worried about something. What if something happened to her?"

"Let's not jump to any conclusions. We have no idea how old the bones are or even if they're human."

"But what if they are?" Aury persisted.

"What are the chances anyone would be buried in a location the clues led us to? Besides, Sarah was still alive when her mother wrote the clues, and it sounds like Mary was still alive when Sarah wrote the note."

"Good point, so what are the chances *anyone* would be buried where the clues led us? Mary wouldn't have her kids digging up an old grave."

"Then it's a good guess the person—"

"If it's a person," Aury interjected.

"If it's a person, they were put in the ground after the clues." Aury stood. "I can't just sit here. What can we work on?"

Scott lifted his chin in the direction of a nearby pile of logs. "Have you ever used a wood splitter?"

Several hours later, Aury heard the voices of men before she saw them round the bend in the road. She and Scott removed their work gloves and walked out to meet them.

"You Scott Bell?" one officer asked.

"I am." Scott offered his hand. "This is Aury St. Clair."

"I'm Detective Hanson. This is Detective Bristine. We're from the Surry County Police Department. Heard you found something interesting."

Scott relayed what they found. "We can walk, but it's quicker if we hop into the maintenance cart." He removed some buckets, leaving a shovel and adding a tarp.

Aury climbed into the back and allowed the officers to sit in the seats where they wouldn't make a mess of their suits.

"Why were you digging around?" Hanson asked.

Scott appeared a little sheepish. "We're sort of on a treasure hunt."

"A treasure hunt?" That got Bristine's attention.

"We found an old diary in the manor," Aury explained. "We were following the clues Mary Townsend left for her children."

"To a treasure?" Hanson said.

"We don't know what's at the end of the hunt," Scott said. "We were just following it for fun. Until we found the bones."

"It may be nothing," Aury added. "We don't know what human bones look like."

They pulled up to the tree line. "We need to walk from here." Scott got out of the truck and picked up the shovel. "This way."

They walked single file through the path to the area along the riverbank where they had been digging. Scott started to insert the shovel and thought better of it.

"Let me." Aury got down and removed the loose dirt with her hands. When it was deep enough to reveal the small bones, she sat on her haunches. "What do you think?"

Bristine braced his hands on his knees as he bent down to examine the find. Standing upright, he turned to Hanson. "Go ahead and call in the techs. They look way too old for this to be an active crime scene, but we better let them collect as much evidence as possible. Maybe we can figure out who this was."

Scott covered the hole with the tarp, and they all pitched in to find rocks and branches heavy enough to weigh down the edges.

Chapter 30

S arah, tell Frederick I don't have to clean the chicken coop," Thomas said as he stormed into the kitchen.

Sarah, elbow-deep in kneading the dough for a vegetable pie she had planned for dinner, continued her work until Frederick appeared. Pausing, she addressed her brother. "Cleaning the coop is your chore. Why are you trying to get Thomas to do it?"

Frederick puffed out his chest. "I'm busy taking inventory and planning where we should put the beehives."

"You said I could help with that!" Thomas complained.

"You will. But I have to figure out the best place first, then gather the wood. I've been tracking the bees to find their queen. We'll need her to start our honey production."

"I still don't know how you plan on doing this without getting stung," Sarah said.

"Father showed me. Smoke from a burning branch will put them to sleep."

"Great. You'll undoubtedly catch the woods on fire. Then where will we be?"

"I can hold the fire," Thomas offered.

Sarah smiled at him. "You help him, Thomas. But for now,

go feed the chickens. Frederick, it's your job to clean the coop. No more bee chasing until that's done."

Frederick stomped out of the kitchen with Thomas happily following on his heels.

Sarah turned to the pie crust, taking out her frustrations on the helpless dough. She didn't know how her mother put up with this every day. No, every hour! The boys were constantly squabbling, and Emily required more attention than Sarah thought possible. The only time she got a chance to read was when tucking them all in at night. And then she had to read the stories they wanted, not the books Father had given her.

As the familiar sounds of the baby stirring from her nap made their way into the kitchen, Sarah put the last touches on the dough, draping it over the pie tin as her mother had taught her. She rinsed her hands and went to get Emily out of bed.

Chapter 31

Present Day

Approaching Eastover, Aury pulled up to the new bridge that had been constructed where the road caved in. As she contemplated whether it was safe to drive across, another sedan drove over the bridge on the way out.

The driver waved to Aury as he passed. She waved back and held her breath as she started over the temporary structure.

Safely on the other side, she exhaled.

Scott was outside the cabin talking to the investigator when she pulled up.

"Afternoon, Aury. You're just in time. Detective Hanson was getting ready to tell me what they found." Scott motioned her to join them.

The lanky man nodded at her. "As I was saying, you were right. They're very old bones. It will take a while for the lab to finish the tests, but I'd guess over one hundred years. It's hard to pinpoint the exact age. Female. That's all we can tell for now. A forensic anthropologist from the College of William and Mary is studying them for more detail now."

"Did you find any other remains?" Jackie asked.

"No. We dug a wide hole around the area, then explored outward using ground-penetrating radar. We only found one skeleton, and it wasn't buried very deep."

Aury looked at Scott. "Do you think it could be Mary?"

"Who's Mary?" Hanson asked.

"She's the writer of the diary we've been reading. For some reason, her diary just stops in 1862, and we don't know why," Scott explained.

"It would be helpful if we could see the diary. When the identity is suspected, we may be able to do a DNA analysis on a living relative."

Aury was excited. "Scott, you could be related. This property has been in your family for generations."

He shrugged. "Sure, you can look at the diary, but I'd like to get it returned eventually. Aury has convinced me of its importance."

"We can make copies and give you the original." Hanson pulled out his notebook. "We also found two slugs. That's one of the reasons we think the skeleton's so old. The researchers at the college call it a Minié ball. It was made from soft lead in the mid-1800s. Used by both sides in the Civil War. But the most interesting find was an old photograph."

"Photograph?"

"Well, more like a small rectangle of silver with a picture in it. It's hard to make it out, but the folks from the college would like your permission to try to clean it up."

"Absolutely," Scott said. "Why would it be with the skeleton?"

"Could be she was carrying it. It was wrapped in oilskin, which preserved the leather case. The photo was under glass. That's the only thing that kept it from being totally destroyed. We don't know much more than that."

"That would fit with the time period of the diary. Scott, this is so exciting." Aury couldn't contain her enthusiasm.

Scott laughed at her. "I'll grab that diary for you," he told the detective.

Aury's mind raced. Why would Mary be buried at one of the

sites of her treasure hunt? Who was in the picture?

Returning from the cabin, Scott handed two journals to Hanson. "Will I get the photo back as well?"

"Of course. It's your property. We appreciate the support. The college folks are enjoying solving a mystery that falls within their areas of expertise. I'd be surprised if someone doesn't write a paper on the find for their senior thesis."

Scott smiled. "Glad something good is coming out of all this."

Hanson shook hands with Scott, then Aury. "We won't be too much longer. The professor is still sniffing around."

After he left, Aury and Scott stood silently, taking in all the information.

"When can we start looking for the next clue?" Aury said.

"Let's go see what they're doing at the site," Scott suggested.

After a short ride to the tree line, they parked next to two other vehicles. At the water's edge, the area was roped off with sticks holding barricade tape.

"At least it doesn't say crime scene," Scott said.

Four people were digging around the hole; two of them in their early twenties wore William and Mary T-shirts. Aury guessed they were college students. An older, dark-skinned woman spotted them and headed their way.

"I'm Doctor Vinson from the Anthropology Department at the college."

The three shook hands. "Garrett and Beth are two of my grad students," she said. Hearing their names, the younger members of the group acknowledged Scott and Aury with a quick wave. "Robert is from the sheriff's office." The fourth in the party gave a nod as he continued his effort.

"Thanks for coming out," Scott said.

"Thank you for letting us. This is a rare find and a wonderful hands-on opportunity for our students."

"I would think it's unusual to find a body buried in the middle of nowhere," Scott said.

"Well, that in and of itself isn't unusual. In the old days, people buried their dead anywhere they had space. They didn't have specific rules about graveyards."

"What are they doing now?" Aury asked, watching the students bag items.

"They're collecting anything that might have significance to this finding. They place it in bags and mark where it was found, how deep, and the like. Anything that can help us determine a date for your skeleton."

Vinson turned to Beth. "Bring me that tin box you found."

An unspoken question passed between Scott and Aury.

"I thought this was odd because it was buried under the body. I guess it could have been trash washed up by the river, but in the 1800s, things like this were usually reused, not discarded so easily."

Beth handed the bag to Scott. "Did you open it?" he asked.

"No. We don't do that until we get everything to the lab," Beth said.

"Is there a reason? Can I open it now?"

Vinson shrugged. "It belongs to you. It isn't historically significant. The tin looks common place. What are you expecting to find?"

Aury explained their treasurer hunt. Vinson was intrigued.

"Sounds like fun. Have you found anything valuable so far?"

"No. We were digging for the treasure here, but I think we may have just found the next clue instead," Aury said.

"Do you need me to wear gloves or anything?" Scott asked the sheriff's deputy.

"It's been buried quite a while. There's nothing of significance about it," he answered.

Scott opened the bag and pulled out the tin. He tapped it against the heel of his shoe to loosen the rust. Prying it open, he found a tile of wood. He flipped it over, tilting it one way, then the other to catch the right light.

"There's something there, but it's too faint to see." Scott handed it to Aury. "Can you make it out?"

"We'll have to check under the magnifying glass."

"I'll do you one better. Why don't you come by the lab, and we'll look at it under the microscope?" Vinson offered.

"Really? That would be great," Aury said. She put the tile in the tin. "When can we go?"

Vinson laughed. "How about meeting up with us next week? We still have some work to do here. We've searched about one hundred yards in each direction, except for the water, of course. Did you know there used to be a building here? We found something similar to stone footings."

"My grandmother thinks it might have been a springhouse," Aury said.

"What I can't figure out is why someone would bury a body near where food was stored. It's not logical," Scott said.

"Maybe it wasn't buried. Could be the person just died there and was left. Especially if it was during the war," Dr. Vinson said.

"You have maps from here?" Beth asked.

"Aury found some in the library archives," Scott said.

"That will save us a lot of time if you're willing to share with us," the professor said.

"Of course. I'll bring them when we visit."

They set a date and location, and Scott and Aury left the researchers to their work.

Chapter 32

May 21, 1862

Mary stepped out of the wagon, pleasantly surprised to find four shining faces there to greet her. "What are you doing here?"

The kids ran to their mother and wrapped their arms around her. She kissed them all in turn and held them tight.

The driver unloaded a basket of provisions from the wagon, placing them behind the huddled group.

"Let me look at you." Mary pretended to be sizing them up. She scooped Emily into her arms. "Oh, you are getting so big!" Emily squealed in delight.

"Sarah, you must be feeding them well. Look how tall the boys are growing!"

Two beaming smiles answered her.

"We will carry the basket for you, Mother," Thomas said. He and Frederick each grabbed a handle.

Mary slipped her free arm around Sarah's shoulders as they walked. "I know this is hard on you. You are doing well, though. I'm very proud."

Sarah leaned into her mother's side. "It's tiring. I'm sorry for all the trouble I caused you growing up."

Mary laughed. "You aren't trouble. It's part of being a

mother, and I love every minute of it. I wouldn't be the same without all of you."

"Are Father and Noah ever coming home?" Sarah whispered so the boys wouldn't overhear. Emily's face turned expectantly to her mother at the mention of her father.

Contemplating the best answer, Mary took her time. Finally, she resorted to the truth without a sugar coating. "I don't think so."

Sarah nodded slightly. Wiping her tears away, she put on a brave face. "Thanks for being honest with me. I won't tell the boys."

"It isn't that he wouldn't return if he could. I just have a bad feeling." Mary couldn't keep her voice from cracking.

Sarah gave her mother a squeeze. "It's okay. We'll get through this."

As they walked, Mary started singing one of their favorite songs. All the kids joined in. Even Emily clapped along.

Chapter 33

Present Day

Scott picked Aury up at her grandmother's house just after lunch. It was an overcast day, threatening rain.

"So nice to finally meet you, Scott," Gran said. "I'm glad to hear Eastover is still going. It's a wonderful service you provide."

"Thank you, Mrs. St. Clair, but honestly I don't know how much longer I'll be able to keep it running. Maybe the new owners will continue it as a retreat center."

"Do you have buyers?" Aury asked.

"No, not yet. I don't want to show it until I can get everything cleaned up from the hurricane."

"That will give you time to find the treasure," Gran said, taking the words out of Aury's mouth. They smiled at each other.

Scott shook his head. "The Townsend family's idea of treasure and what I need to finance this place are potentially two very different things. You'll have to come for a visit, Mrs. St. Clair."

"Call me Liza, dear. I would love to come by some time. Thank you."

Aury kissed her grandmother's cheek. "When we're done at the college, Scott is going to drive me to Eastover to deal with my car. Hopefully I'll get it today with no issues."

Gran patted her hand. "Be careful. Another storm is brewing."

As they drove to William and Mary, Aury pondered the mystery. "What do you think they would have considered a treasure in the 1860s?"

"Real silverware, I'd think. Jewelry, of course."

"Land?"

Scott thought about it. "Sure, but it has to be something they could bury, and I already have the deed to Eastover."

They lapsed into thought through the rest of the drive.

At the college, Scott pulled into a visitor's spot near Washington Hall. Dr. Vinson met them at the door to the lab.

"Glad you could make it in," she said. "Would you like a quick tour of the lab?"

"That would be fun," Aury said.

Dr. Vinson walked them through the vast space, crowded with tables, working students, and various equipment. She stopped at one table to introduce a graduate student.

"Lacey, this is Scott and Aury. Can you tell them what you're working on?"

Lacey stood and shook their hands. "I'm working in historical biology, looking at biological effects of diverse social conditions."

"Wow," Scott said. "That's a mouthful. And a lot more detail than I ever considered in college."

Aury smiled. "Pretty impressive."

She showed them a line of bony growth on a leg bone she had been studying. "I'm looking at enlarged muscle attachments on a femur in this population to see how hard they worked. The larger the attachment, the greater the persistent strain on the muscle." She put the bone on the table. "These people had been enslaved, and their muscles were clearly working hard."

"That's amazing," Aury said. "I didn't know you could tell that much from bones."

"Lacey may want to examine the skeleton we found on your

property. Her findings may help us identify who she was," Dr. Vinson said.

They thanked Lacey and followed Dr. Vinson to an empty seat in front of a microscope. Scott handed her the wooden tile which she placed under the lens. After making some slight adjustments, she moved aside to make room for Scott to look.

Aury pulled her notebook from her purse, preparing to write what Scott saw.

Under the bright light and magnification, the indents in the wood were easier to read, even where the ink had faded.

Scott read while Aury scribbled his words.

"Near the—something I can't make out—where stands the first something-something—I think it says stone," Scott said.

"Lies a patch of garden, oft left alone. Peel back the—something—green and fair to reveal the next clue buried there."

"I can't make out all of it. Do you want to try?" Scott relinquished his seat to Aury.

She slid in place and readjusted the tile under the lens. "I think you're right. That last word in the first line is stone. I can't make out the third line."

"The biology department has a scanning electron microscope. Let's try that," Dr. Vinson said.

A short walk through campus brought them to the Integrated Science Center. Dr. Vinson conferred with another faculty member while Scott and Aury waited. Moments later, they stood in front of a machine with a computer monitor. Dr. Vinson placed the wood sample under the lens, and an enlarged image of the writing was projected on the screen.

Aury was surprised at how clear the writing had become. "Yes, it definitely says stone, and the missing word in the third line is ivy."

Scott looked at the words Aury had written. "Makes sense too."

"I'm still not sure about the first line. The third word looks short, but it's still too faint."

"You got me." Turning to Dr. Vinson, he said, "Thanks for

all your help with our puzzle."

"We'll have students put your skeleton together over the next few days to see if we have all the parts. We have the skull, which will make it easier to narrow down our search." Dr. Vinson escorted Scott and Aury out of the building.

They thanked her again and walked to Scott's car.

Aury was too excited to sit quietly on their drive to Eastover. "What stone do you think it's referencing?"

"Hard to say. They used stones for everything during those times."

"What about stones they used to get into carriages?" Aury said.

"They were simple farmers. Not sure they'd have carriage steps, but we could check near the manor house."

"I don't remember seeing anything like that, but I wasn't looking for it either."

"It might have been moved or repurposed for something else," Scott said. "More likely they would have something closer to the barn for climbing on horses."

He smiled. "My grandparents had a pony when I was little. I remember fighting with my cousins over who got to ride first."

"Are you still close with your cousins?"

"Not so much. They're married with kids."

"You don't like kids?" Aury asked.

He took his eyes off the road long enough to glance at her. "I love kids. It just hasn't been in my cards."

She smiled. "What does that mean?"

He blew out his breath. "I worked long hours trying to establish myself. Then my mom got sick, then dad."

"Sorry, I wasn't thinking." Aury felt horrible teasing about something so personal.

Scott shrugged it off.

"And I have you on some wild treasure hunt."

"That's my favorite part. It's a welcome distraction from the work I need to do." He gave her another sideways look. "I deserve some downtime."

"Yes, you do."

A broad smile lit his face. "Besides, I need the money."

They lapsed into a comfortable, thoughtful silence. As they approached the turn off for the retreat center, Aury said, "I let the other ladies know you said they could pick up their cars today."

"Thanks. Let's go out to the motel and make sure everything is cleared away."

When they pulled up in front of the building, the quilters were already gathered around.

"Hey, stranger." Deb wrapped Aury in a bear hug. "Glad to see he hasn't worked you to death," she said with a glance toward Scott.

Linda also hugged Aury while Suzanne waited her turn.

"Carla and Pat are coming up later," Deb said. "We couldn't wait to see how everything looked after the storm."

"That bridge is a little nerve wracking," Linda said.

"It's only temporary," Scott assured her. "When things calm down a bit, I'll have contractors come in and repair the road."

Suzanne nodded to the pile of debris. "How did you move the trees away from our cars?"

"Cut them up with a chainsaw, then used the tractor to drag the pieces away. Time consuming but effective. We'll have a massive bonfire later."

"Can we get the rest of the stuff out of our rooms?" Deb asked.

"Not out of the rooms on the side where the trees hit, sorry. I still need someone to come in and check the structural integrity. I don't want anyone hurt."

"Good thing we packed as much as we could in the cars before we left," Linda said.

As they chatted, the tow truck pulled in to haul away the damaged car.

"I have some work to do," Scott told them.

"I'll come by a little later, if that's okay with you," Aury said. "I want to walk around here a bit."

"Okay. I'll be at the dining hall trying to plan out my next list of chores."

When the driver emerged from the truck, Suzanne said, "Thanks for coming out."

"Sorry it took so long. We've been busy after the hurricane," the driver said.

"Any idea how long it will take to look it over?"

"The mechanics are expecting it; they'll start as soon as I bring it in. If the alignment is okay and the engine turns over, you should have it today. If there's more damage, they'll give you a better estimate." He gestured at the dent near the wheel well. "I'm going to have to pull that out before I can tow your car, so it doesn't rub on the tire."

While the ladies watched the driver work, Aury went to the room she had occupied during the retreat. It was far from the nearest downed tree, therefore still in one piece. The rotting odor of musty air assaulted her nostrils as she opened the door. Without air conditioning to keep it at bay, the dampness of the old building was taking over.

Breathing through her mouth, Aury gathered all her belongings from the room and put them inside her car. She rolled the windows down to air out the small space.

By the time she finished, the others were ready to head out. The ladies split up and started their cars. Deb and Suzanne were going to follow the tow truck to the garage.

Aury drove her car to the manor house to look for carriage stones, her mind working the puzzle. As she approached the once-stately building, she was struck again by sadness that the building had fallen into such disrepair.

Starting at the front of the house, Aury walked straight across the driveway, head down, searching for a stone. At the edge where the grass met the dirt, a tuft of taller green criss-crossed itself.

Aury dropped to her knees, pushing the grass aside. A flat gray stone lay almost level with the ground. The second stone that would have at one time rested upon it was gone. She stood and searched around the grassy area but found no other stone.

She went to the front porch and sat on the top step. It was so peaceful, Aury felt she could fall asleep on this spot. Then the wheels in her head started turning again. Looking around, she tried to spot something that could have been a patch of garden.

Getting to her feet, she walked around the house. Off the kitchen was an area that had obviously been set aside at one time as a garden. She would have to ask Scott how long that chicken wire fence had been there.

Finding nothing else substantial that looked like a garden, she went to see what Scott was working on.

Chapter 34

June 4, 1862

Thomas, quit pestering Frederick. You don't like it when he does that to you," Sarah scolded. She glanced anxiously up the dirt road. Her mother's wagon should have arrived by now.

Emily squirmed to be let down. Sarah placed her in the grass where she could chase butterflies.

"Where is she?" Frederick asked.

"How should I know?" Sarah snapped. She reached out her hand to her brother. "I'm sorry. I'm worried, that's all."

Normally Frederick wouldn't have even considered holding his sister's hand, but today was an exception. He gave it a small squeeze.

"I'm hungry." Thomas bounded up to them.

Frederick dropped his sister's hand and gave Thomas a playful shove. "You're always hungry."

"Did you bring food?" Thomas looked up hopefully at Sarah.

She glanced down the empty road again. The sun was setting, and she didn't want to be out after dark. "Let's head back."

"But Momma—" Frederick started.

"Knows her way," Sarah finished before an argument

started. "She'll be more upset if I don't have you all fed and in bed at a reasonable hour."

Slowly, the small band of children headed for home. Frederick dragged his feet, and Sarah knew it was because he hoped their mother would catch up with them.

By the time they reached the porch steps, Emily had fallen asleep on Sarah's shoulder. *She is getting too big to be carried,* Sarah thought as she gently laid her on the divan in the sitting room. When she entered the kitchen, Frederick had pulled out the last of the bread and began cutting it into small chunks.

He handed the largest piece to Thomas. "Don't shovel it into your mouth all at once."

Thomas looked at his brother with defiance and took a large bite.

Frederick rolled his eyes and handed a piece to Sarah. She took the apple butter from the cupboard and spread it on her bread, then passed it to Frederick.

"Hey, I want some," Thomas said.

"Then you shouldn't have eaten all your bread at once," Frederick answered.

Sarah tore off some of her bread, added jam, and gave it to Thomas who licked off the jam before eating it.

"I'll make bread tomorrow. I need you two to bring in more firewood for the oven." She made a mental note to check the springhouse to see what was left. Although the cool water from the James River helped extend the life of some foods, it had been a while since their mother had the time to make preserves.

"Perhaps we'll go berry picking tomorrow as well. We can have fruit biscuits for Sunday breakfast." Sarah put the lid on the jam, placing it on the counter. "Now, you two, wash your face and get in bed. Thomas, I'll know if you don't wash."

Frederick ushered Thomas from the room. Sarah sank into one of the chairs. Tears welled in her eyes as she tried not to think about her mother. What if, just like Father, she didn't come home? She crossed her arms on the table and rested her forehead.

Chapter 35

Present Day

"Scott said there's been a kitchen garden in the same spot for as long as he can remember," Aury told her grandmother as they sipped their coffee in Gran's small kitchen.

"But you said it isn't within sight of the carriage stones. I don't think that's what she could be referring to. Besides, why would the carriage stones be 'the first stone'?"

"Maybe there's another set of carriage stones," Aury said.

"They're usually only by the house where carriages would stop. What other buildings are on the property?"

"A few smaller cottages, but they were built a lot later. I think Scott said his grandparents built them to rent out and for the groundskeeper."

"What about other gardens?"

"The Townsends had a few crops, but not that last year. According to Mary's diary, they didn't plant because James was gone."

"What about a flower garden? You said Mary Townsend came from a more well-to-do family. She might have appreciated something frivolous to remind her of home," Gran suggested.

"There's no telling where that might be now."

"Maybe the Master Gardeners could help you again." Gran

got up to get another cup of coffee.

"This is my first day back to work," Aury said. "I might be able to go over to their offices during lunch."

"You don't sound excited," Gran teased her.

"I'd much rather be treasure hunting. It's hard to get motivated to look at spreadsheets and balanced budgets when the Eastover treasure is calling me."

"I don't think you could make a career of treasure hunting, though. The accounting firm pays your bills."

"I know, but I can dream, can't I?" She looked at her watch. Taking a last drink from her coffee, she placed the mug in the sink and kissed her grandmother's cheek.

"I'll check in on you later," Aury said.

"I'm fine. You worry too much."

"We'll at least make a grocery run. I need to pick up a few things too."

Gran waved as Aury dashed out the door.

Time dragged on as Aury checked her watch every five minutes, waiting for her lunch break. She had called ahead to Eleanor and arranged to meet the couple at their office.

"How lovely to see you again," Keith said, standing to greet Aury when she arrived.

"Would you like some coffee?" Eleanor offered.

"No, thank you. I don't have much time before I need to get to work."

"So you found another clue?" Eleanor asked.

Aury pulled a piece of paper from her pocket and handed it to the older woman.

Eleanor read it so Keith could hear.

> *Near the path where stands the first blank stone*
> *Lies a patch of garden, oft left alone.*

Peel back the ivy, green and fair,
To reveal the next clue, buried there."

"Did you find the first stone?" Keith said.

"No. We aren't sure what that is. We thought it might be a carriage stone, but the kitchen garden isn't within sight of the front of the house."

"It wouldn't be a kitchen garden," Eleanor said. "It says 'oft left alone.' A kitchen garden would be visited constantly."

"Good point. Gran thought maybe a flower garden."

"It'll be hard to identify a garden after so much time has passed," Eleanor said.

"I think you'll do better looking for the stone. Are there any places on the property where there's a buildup of stones?" Keith asked.

"The old barn, but we already found a clue there. I don't think she'd hide two things in one location. Besides, how would we know which one was the first stone?"

"Buildings have a cornerstone. That's the first stone put down that sets the boundary for where the other stones are placed," Keith said.

"Why didn't I think of that?" Aury said. "That's brilliant. So it would be on the corner of the building. I'll check again."

"I can't imagine they would plant a flower garden right next to the stables, though. Usually they wouldn't put anything tempting to eat so close to the horses," Eleanor said.

"Any other place with stones?" Keith asked.

Something niggled at Aury's thoughts. She remembered seeing a large stone somewhere that looked like it was out of place to her.

"In the woods!" she exclaimed when it came to her. "I was walking through the woods, and I found a large stone tipped over on its side. It was about this tall." She placed her hand two feet off the ground. "And it was unnaturally square."

"That sounds like a boundary stone," Keith said. "They were used to outline the borders of property."

"Would there be more than one?" Aury said.

"Sure, so there must be a first one. They're often numbered. Try searching the front of the property, near where the road would have been. Not necessarily where it is now."

"It would make more sense to have a flower garden not often visited near the road where people passing by would see and admire it," Eleanor said.

Aury was elated. She felt like they had made a breakthrough. Glancing at her watch, she stood. "I need to run. Thanks again for your help."

As soon as she left the office, she texted Scott. She realized he wouldn't receive her message until he went into town and could get a signal, but she wanted to let him know she might have a lead.

Chapter 36

That night as Aury pored over the maps she had copied from the library, Scott called. She filled him in on her conversation with the gardeners.

"What do you think? Could they be boundary stones?" Aury asked.

"I don't see why not. Are the locations on any of the maps you have?"

"No, but I do have a few that show boundary lines and old roads. We can start by looking there."

"Sounds good. I'm in town now picking up supplies, and I have to meet with some contractors tomorrow. Maybe you can come over for dinner after that, and we can walk the property before it gets dark," Scott suggested.

"I'll be there. I'll even bring dessert."

They hung up and Aury went back to her maps, meticulously comparing them to modern day maps on her phone, then making notations on her copies. The boundary had changed a few times over the many years, but she thought she had a good idea where to start their search.

As promised, Aury arrived in time for dinner with a fresh apple pie. "Gran said this is her contribution to our treasure hunt," Aury said, setting the pie on the picnic table.

"Are you hungry now or should we investigate first?" Scott asked.

"Investigate. I want to see if my maps are close to what is currently here."

Aury grabbed her bag of maps and notes, and they rode the utility cart to where the main road passed by the Eastover property.

Scott turned the vehicle around as Aury oriented the maps to the way they were facing. "This road isn't on the 1850s maps." Aury pointed at the line she had penciled in to represent the current entrance to Eastover. "It looks like the old road was another hundred or so yards in and to the left of this road."

Scott drove down the path until Aury told him to stop. "There used to be a structure of some sort here," she said.

They got out of the vehicle and walked in parallel lines fifty yards apart in the direction of the original road. Only veering off their course to move around trees or bushes, Aury and Scott kept their eyes pinned to the ground.

"This is too far. Why don't we shift that way a bit?" Scott followed her directions as they moved farther from the entrance and continued, once again walking fifty yards apart.

"Aury, come here. I think I found something." Scott dropped to his knees and pulled at the vines and brush covering a gray square block.

"That looks like the one I found in the woods! Is there a number on it?"

Scott swept his hands over the stone, clearing away more of the dirt. "This looks like a Z."

Aury dropped down beside him. "Probably a two. Curves might have been hard to carve."

He looked closer. "You're right. We should be close. Any idea how far apart the boundary stones were usually set?"

"No, but if this is where the road came through, it might be on the other side of the path. Let's keep going."

They spread out again and walked deeper into the property, away from where they parked the cart.

This time Aury stumbled across the marker. Scott joined her and they pulled away the growth. "Definitely a one!" Aury beamed, the excitement of discovery spiking her adrenaline.

"Now we have to find a garden," Scott said, looking around at the trees and bushes nearby.

"Do you smell that?" Aury asked.

Scott sniffed the air. "Honeysuckle?"

"I think so." Aury followed her nose and came upon a patch of wild and unkempt rose bushes. "They're beautiful."

"What are these purple flowers?" Scott said.

"Asters. Gran used to have them in her garden. They're hardy plants and need little maintenance."

"I think we found the garden," Scott said. "Now what?"

"The clue says to peel back the ivy. After all this time, who knows? There's ivy all over the place."

"I think that's the spread of the ivy. Where would a gardener plant ivy to begin with?"

"It would need some type of support, like a trellis or fence." Aury looked around. "Anything wood is long gone."

They expanded their search from the roses, walking toward the thickest patch of honeysuckle.

"Aury, look here." Scott motioned to the ground where a low rise of rocks created a miniature wall.

"Makes sense. Mary would have surrounded her little oasis garden with something."

They followed the outline of the perimeter, surprised that so much of it was still intact. There was a five-foot area where there was no trace of a wall.

"Maybe she had an arbor here going over the entry to the garden." Aury outlined an archway with her arms.

"Even so, where would we dig?"

Aury kicked in the growth. Her foot slid across something smooth. With a little more effort, she uncovered a flat, oval rock resting flush with the ground.

She scanned the immediate area. "I don't see anything else like this. It was probably placed here."

"I'll go get the shovel."

A few minutes later, Scott returned. Placing the tip of the shovel under the rock, he pried it away from the dirt. Minutes later, he was digging at the moist ground beneath.

After ten minutes, he stopped. "I don't think this is the place. She wouldn't have buried it too deep."

"I think it's the right place. Maybe they just found the treasure already."

"But why would all the other clues still be in place?" Scott wondered aloud.

Aury shivered. The day had been warm, but the heat had left with the setting sun. "Let's go eat. I left my jacket in the car."

Scott refilled the hole and shifted the rock into place.

At the cabin, he started a fire in the pit and put a cast-iron pot on a hanger above it to warm.

"That had to be the right spot," Aury said, poking at the fire with a stick. "Everything else fit the clue."

"Someone totally unrelated might have found whatever was buried, not even knowing about the other clues."

Aury felt the disappointment weigh her down. She didn't understand why it mattered so much to her that they find the treasure—whatever it was. It wasn't like she had a claim to it, but she was hoping it could help Scott out of the financial burden Eastover had become. And, if she was being honest with herself, she didn't want him to have to sell and leave the area. She'd miss him.

The setback was heartrending.

As if reading her thoughts, Scott said, "Guess I need to find another way to pay the taxes on this place."

She gave him a wan smile.

Chapter 37

June 5, 1862

Sarah walked along the bank of the river toward the spring-house. It was a beautiful day with a slight breeze. She hummed a song she had heard her mother sing many times as she tucked them in at night.

Voices interrupted her tune. She dashed to the rear of the small building and hid from sight. More clearly now, voices drifted across the water. She peeked above the roof and saw soldiers on a raft. She ducked down again to wait until they passed.

Sitting on a rock behind the springhouse, she was reminded of the treasure hunt their mother had fashioned for them. One of the clues led here. She poked with a stick until she found the marker her mother had placed there to show them where to dig. *I'll need to move this clue further from the river*, she thought. *We don't want a soldier to find it.*

Eventually the raft rounded the bend, and Sarah went to the front of the building. She moved aside the driftwood and brambles she and Frederick had placed there to hide the wooden structure from the river. Although dark and musty, Sarah loved the feel of the cool room. It was like a secret hideout with fresh water gurgling through the structure.

She slipped inside and held the door open just far enough to let in sunlight to see by. She counted the jars on the shelf, grabbing one jam and picking up a head of cabbage. Backing out, she fastened the door and replaced the foliage.

When she heard sounds of gunfire, she swiftly moved up the bank and melted into the trees.

Chapter 38

Present Day

W e were able to find most of a full skeleton," Dr. Vinson said when she had Scott and Aury in front of the exam table.

In their disappointment over not finding the treasure, they had almost forgotten about their other find. When Dr. Vinson reached out to Scott, he had set up a time when both he and Aury could stop by the college to hear what she had uncovered. Aury gave up her lunch hour, but it was worth it.

Dr. Vinson pointed to the chest area. "The ribs on the right are mostly intact. The left side is shattered."

"Is that something that could have happened after she died?" Scott asked.

"I doubt it. If something fell on her or the bones at some point after death, they would have broken, but it's not likely they would have shattered. A coroner would be able to tell you more."

A student interrupted their conversation to get guidance from Dr. Vinson.

"Are you ready for the real reason you're here?" Dr. Vinson asked them when she was finished.

"Sure," Scott said.

She escorted them to another lab down the hall. "They've been working on your daguerreotype."

"Our what?" Aury asked.

Dr. Vinson smiled. "Daguerreotype. It's a way of taking a photograph used in the early 1800s. A highly polished silver surface was attached to a copper surface, then exposed to iodine fumes to make it sensitive to light. The plate was put in a camera. After exposing it to light, the photo was developed with mercury vapor."

"Quite the process," Scott said.

"It was the first commercial photographic process. They're very delicate and easily damaged. Yours was in a protective case, so it fared better than most."

Dr. Vinson opened the door to the lab for them. "Stanley, these are the owners of the daguerreotype."

Aury pointed at Scott. "He is. I'm just along for the mystery."

Dr. Stanley Ross shook hands with them. "Great find. Thanks for sharing with us. Would you like to see it so far?"

"Yes," Scott and Aury said in unison.

He escorted them to a workstation where the photograph was inside a protective enclosure. "We have to wait for new glass to be cut so we can reassemble the photo and reseal it. We don't want any further damage done to the picture inside. I wanted to show you what we found when we took the dag frame from the case."

He picked up a yellowed piece of paper and handed it to Scott. "Does this mean something to you?"

Scott read,

> *"When you are searching for more*
> *And there is grass beneath your toes*
> *You know where to look.*
> *Just follow your nose."*

Scott shook his head. "One more thing for us to figure out, I guess."

They said their good-byes and left Dr. Ross to his work. As

they walked out of the college building, Aury's mind struggled to piece out the new clue.

"Searching for more what?" she said.

"Flowers? It says follow your nose," Scott offered.

"But she already hid something in the flower garden. She wouldn't send them to the same place again."

"There must have been more than one garden. But how does this clue point us to a particular one?"

"Grass beneath your toes? That just tells me it's outside. Where else would a garden be?"

"Good point. Maybe it isn't a garden. What can be outside or inside?"

"The outhouse?" Scott said.

"Yikes. Following your nose would fit for that, but not 'when you're searching for more.' If you want more, it's a good smell, right?"

They reached Aury's car, and she leaned against it. "I've been doing some internet searches on birth and death records from the 1800s. There has been a law on the books as early as 1632 that required ministers to record births and deaths. Virginia passed a law in 1853 that put it in the hands of the commissioner of revenue."

"Leave it up to the tax organization to make sure they account for every penny," Scott said.

Aury smiled her agreement. "Now those records are in the state archives in Richmond. I thought I'd drive up there on Friday and see what's available."

"What are you looking for specifically?"

"James, Noah, and Mary didn't return to Eastover, as far as we can tell."

"Unless the skeleton is Mary's," Scott pointed out.

Aury agreed. "But at least I might be able to find something about James and Noah."

"I'll leave you to the book research. I have to touch base with my office this week, so they know I'm still on the payroll."

Aury straightened up, and Scott opened her door for her. "When are you coming out to Eastover?" he asked.

"I was hoping to bring Gran out on Friday. Does that work for you?"

"Sounds perfect. See you then."

After he walked away, Aury sat in her car and made a list of questions she wanted answers to. What happened to James and Noah? She assumed they died, or they would have come returned. Maybe they did, but Mary hadn't updated her diary.

A thought struck her. What if they had come back and the treasure was gone? Maybe there was no mystery at all. As she turned this over in her mind, she felt silly. She had gotten excited over nothing.

She jotted down more things on her list.

> *Check the family Bible for death records*
> *Check Surry County oldest church records*
> *Cemetery headstones?*
> *Military records for James or Noah*

She set her pen aside and stared out the window into the dark. What had happened to the kids? She picked up her pen and added another item.

> *Death records for all the kids*

Friday, Aury picked Gran up after lunch for their trip to Richmond.

"How did you wrangle another day off?" Gran asked.

"I worked this morning. It was scheduled as a half-day because some of the employees are going to a conference in northern Virginia, and they wanted a head start on traffic."

As they waited for the archivist to bring them the material

they had requested, Gran took in the architecture of the library.

"A little too modern for my taste," she said.

"Thanks for coming with me, Gran."

Gran patted her hand. "I love the chance to visit Richmond. I don't do it near often enough anymore."

"We should make it a point to come up at least monthly. There's plenty to do here. They even have a quilt show in October each year."

"Let's do that," Gran agreed.

"Here you go," the archivist said, handing over a number of volumes and three spools of microfiche. "Do you know how to use the machine?"

"Yes, thank you," Aury replied. "Gran, let's take the room on the right."

The ladies settled into the niche that held a microfiche machine, a small table, and two chairs. While Aury threaded the machine, Gran looked through the books. Soon she was lost in the past.

An hour later, Aury pushed away from the machine. "I searched Surry, York, and James City Counties, but I haven't found anything on James or Noah Townsend."

"Did you try various spellings?"

"Yes, I thought of that. Nothing close."

"What about Mary?"

"There are so many Marys in that period, I'm not sure where to start. Townsend was a common name. There was nothing in Surry or James City Counties, but York County has a short note about a Mary Townsend who died in 1862 of typhoid. No birth date. It lists her as married but doesn't name her husband."

"If she died of typhoid, maybe the kids caught it as well," Gran said.

"But they couldn't have all died of it or Scott wouldn't be a descendent," Aury reasoned. "Did you find anything interesting?"

"Mostly information about land grants and how property was divided, then passed down through the generations. There was one mention of Eastover." She referred to her notes. "It was originally part of a land grant in 1637 from the King of England to Henry Brown. Of course the boundary lines have changed over the centuries, adding and subtracting in places. Now it covers two hundred and eighty-three acres."

"When was the manor house built?"

Gran checked her notes. "1840s. No exact date. Of course, it was much smaller than what it is now."

"Scott said the original didn't have a kitchen inside, so that was added on later. It's over four thousand square feet now."

"Let's go. I'd like to see it while the sun is up," Gran said.

Instead of taking the interstate to Williamsburg, Aury took the country roads leading to Surry County and Eastover.

"Scott said he found the family Bible. The deaths of the two babies were recorded, but no deaths later than that. Not even marriages of any of the children."

"Maybe we need to track Scott's lineage backward. How did he end up with the house?" Gran asked.

"From his grandparents. His dad's side, I think."

"Let's ask him to give us as much information about his relatives that he can remember. Obviously, it was passed out of the Townsend name at some point to end up in the Bell family."

"Wouldn't the property deed have a list of owners? I got copies of those when I was at the library," Aury said.

Gran patted her arm. "That's a wonderful idea. We need to look at the deed records."

When they pulled up in front of Scott's cottage, Gran was eager to explore. "I feel like a young child again, playing in the woods with my sisters."

Scott came from behind the building and greeted them.

"Liza, I'm so glad you were able to visit. I hear you've been helping behind the scenes on our adventure," Scott said, shaking her hand.

"You have a beautiful place. I can see why your grandparents loved it so much."

"I see you have electricity," Aury said.

"Yep. Came on this morning. They cut the power to the motel, of course. I think the best thing to do will be to knock the building down altogether. Not worth salvaging. We'll try to get your stuff out first. What can't be saved will be covered by the insurance."

Aury waved away his concerns. "No one is in a rush. Trust me, quilters always have a stash of fabric and enough equipment to keep sewing."

Scott offered Gran his elbow. "What would you like to see first?"

"I would love to visit the manor house."

"Then let's go." He helped her into the utility cart, and Aury jumped in the back.

On the short ride to the house, Aury pointed out various places she and Scott had found clues. "You got a lot done this week," she commented to Scott.

"The weather has been beautiful, and I'm on a deadline. I have to go to the office next week. I've used up all my vacation time."

An unexpected feeling of sadness hit Aury. This had become her personal getaway and now Scott was leaving. She wasn't sure what she had expected.

They pulled into the circular drive. "It's beautiful," Gran said.

"It needs a lot of work," Scott countered. "I've only had time to replace the rotten wood on the steps and porch."

"Oh, but can't you just picture the way it looked at the turn of the century?" Gran stood with her hands clasped in front of her, admiring the columns on the front porch.

Entering the house, Aury let her grandmother lead the way. She followed along as Gran made appreciative noises over various characteristics of the house.

"We had a dining room table very much like this growing up," Gran said.

They finished their tour in the library. While Gran inspected the books on the shelves, Aury filled Scott in on what they found at the library in Richmond.

"Do you know any of your family history prior to your grandparents?" Aury asked when she finished the account of their findings.

Scott rubbed his neck thoughtfully. "My mom was looking into the history of this place when she got sick. I'll see if I can find her notes. They're at my apartment."

"Where do you live?" Gran asked.

"In Shirlington, Virginia, near DC."

"That's not too far. What do you do?"

Aury was glad Gran was asking the questions, not her. She was curious but didn't want to come across as too interested.

"I'm an engineer at Harrington and Associates. We do a lot of consulting on government contracts. You know, as much as I enjoy my job, I've had more fun the past few weeks working with my hands. Here, I can actually see results from my efforts when I'm chopping up trees or filling in potholes."

"Aury was just saying the same thing to me the other day," Gran said. "She's an accountant, you know."

Aury felt her face grow hot. She knew her grandmother was proud of her, but she didn't want her to do any matchmaking.

"Oh yeah? Maybe I should hire you to look over the books for this place. See if I have any hope of digging myself out," Scott said.

"I'd be happy to help," Aury said.

"You two ready to get out of here? I'll treat you to dinner in town before you have to catch the ferry," Scott said.

Chapter 39

July 1862

As Sarah placed her mother's jewelry in the tin, the memories came flooding in. On special occasions, her mother had let her try on different pieces, telling her the stories of their origin. Many came from Mary's father. Although Sarah had never met him, she knew he was a wealthy man up north. He had visited once, shortly after Frederick was born, but she was too small to remember.

The jewelry had come from Sarah's father as a wedding gift to his bride. The stones weren't as large, but Sarah knew her mother treasured them above all the rest. She picked up the ring her mother always wore. She had left it behind when she went to work in the city. Sarah slipped it on her finger, but it was too big.

She knew someday the jewelry would be hers and Emily's, except for a few items her mother would give to the boys' wives. She used to be excited by the idea. Now, she would give them all away to get her mother back. She took off the ring and placed it with the other items in the tin.

Next, she moved to her father's wardrobe. She had never opened it before. The smell of wood and tree sap evoked a sense of her father's presence as if he'd just come in from felling trees; the sensation almost reduced her to tears. She missed him terribly.

Pulling out a pair of pants, she held them up. She may be able to cuff the bottoms. If he wore suspenders, Frederick could wear these, and Thomas could wear the pants Frederick had outgrown. She looked through the other items and took down some work shirts, placing them on the bed.

At the rear of the wardrobe sat a carved, wooden box. Sarah pulled it out and placed it on the floor. Sitting down beside it, she carefully opened the lid, feeling slightly guilty for snooping. She didn't understand much of the writing on the documents. They were legal in nature, and the words were not common use.

Pushing them aside, she found some gold coins and bits of metal she didn't recognize. Her father was a mystery to her. Although loving and hardworking, he didn't talk about serious things often, so she didn't know much about his past.

She replaced everything in the wooden box, then added her mother's jewelry from the tin. She removed one of her mother's dresses from a hook and wrapped it around the box to protect it. With the soldiers getting closer, anything of value must be hidden so it wouldn't fall into their hands.

Sarah was determined to protect her family the way her mother would have wanted her to. She would leave their valuables where Mother had ended their treasure hunt months ago. No one would find them there unless they knew where to look. Her mother had selected the perfect place.

Chapter 40

Present Day

Scott called Aury the following week. "I found the research my mom did on Eastover. She didn't get very far, but you are welcome to look over it."

"When are you coming down?"

"I'll be there Friday night. I have an appraiser coming out to look over the property."

"Are you thinking about selling?" Aury had an uneasy feeling again.

"I have to consider my options. I hate the idea of losing it, but it isn't a moneymaker as it is. It'll take more money than I have to get it operational again."

"What about a loan?"

"That's why I need the appraisal. I need to see how much collateral it's worth. I only have an apartment here. No house to mortgage."

Aury was quiet as her mind rushed through various possibilities.

"You still there?" Scott asked.

"Yes. Sorry. Would you be willing to consider investors?"

"I'd consider almost anything at this point."

"Let me think about it some more. Why don't you bring

your books for the business when you come? Maybe I can come up with other alternatives."

They made plans to meet on Saturday and disconnected. As Aury sat with her phone in her lap contemplating ideas, the phone rang and startled her.

"Hi, Gran."

"How was work today?"

"Boring. But I was able to put together a list of graveyards in the area. I never did check grave markers like you suggested."

Gran chuckled. "I don't think that's what you're getting paid to do, young lady."

"I know, but this is so much more fun. We saved a lot of time by visiting the library in Richmond."

"Where were Mary's parents from? If something happened to her, maybe her parents took the kids."

"Good idea!" Aury thumbed through her notes. "In her diary, Mary mentioned her father owned a textile company in Philadelphia, Pennsylvania."

"How about I search for the kids' death records?" Gran suggested. "You said two girls and two boys, right? I'll look for marriage records for the girls to see what their last names were changed to."

Aury scribbled notes, not wanting to miss a thread they could follow. She wasn't sure why she was working on this so hard. It wasn't getting them any closer to the treasure Scott so desperately needed. But it may help them solve the mystery of the skeleton by the river.

"I think we should start with the cemeteries in Yorktown first. That's the only reference we found of a Mary who might be our Mary."

"When are you going?" Gran asked.

"Tomorrow after work, I think. Do you want to come with me?"

"Not this time, dear. But call and let me know what you find."

Aury wasn't sure what she should be looking for exactly, but she took her notebook, just in case. When she arrived at the Yorktown National Cemetery, the docent was taking in the sidewalk sign announcing that the visitor's center was open.

"Did you have any questions?" she asked.

"I see you have an M. Townsend listed on your website as being buried here in June of 1862. Do you have any more information about that person?" Aury asked.

"Come on inside and let's take a look."

Aury took in the framed posters and shelves of books lining the walls as she followed the docent.

"Is this a relative of yours?" the elderly woman asked, pulling a book from the shelf.

"Not of mine. I'm trying to track down an ancestor for a friend."

"What military unit was he with?"

"Oh, she wasn't in the military. I found something in the Richmond Library archives that notes a Mary Townsend in Yorktown who died of typhoid, but it doesn't give any more details than that. The only mention of burial I found was here for M. Townsend. Could it be Mary?"

"If she was working in one of the army hospitals, it could be. What year was it again?"

"1862."

The docent ran her gnarled finger down the list of names in a three-ring binder. "M. Townsend. Female. Married. Ah, yes. This makes sense. It is thought she was a nurse in the field hospital at the Thomas Nelson house. They had an epidemic of typhoid run through there in early summer. Killed hundreds of soldiers and civilians alike. No family claimed her, so they would have buried her along with the other unclaimed bodies."

The docent read in silence for a moment. "There's a cross

reference here. There is a Mary Townsend listed in letters written by Private Forrest Redding to his parents."

This time, the helpful woman took her place behind a computer terminal. After typing in a few lines, she scanned the screen, scrolling with her mouse. "Here you go." She gestured for Aury to come around the desk to view the screen. "These letters are dictated just how they were written, so don't mind the misspellings or poor grammar."

Aury read.

> *Dear Parents,*
>
> *I now take this opportunity to asure you I am well. The great battle I found myself in a few days past was the worsed of my Life but I only sufferd the most minor of injurys.*
>
> *A kind woman by the name of Mary Townsend cleaned me up good and says I will be joining my unit again soon. Too be honest, I am not ecited to go back to the tents but I will do what I was sent to do. It wasent much fun to hear them old shell whissing over our heads.*
>
> *Misssus Townsend asked me whether I had seen her husband or son. I was unable to releeve her heart. I seen so many men I canent remember names outside my unit.*
>
> *I must stop   write as soon as you can.*

"Can I get a copy of this?" Aury asked the docent.

"Of course." With a push of a button, Aury heard the printer whir into action. "Did it answer your question?"

"It got us a step closer. It fits with the Mary we know about. In her diary, she states her husband and oldest son leave to go into town, but they didn't come back. I guess she could have worked with the wounded hoping to learn something."

"Typhoid was rampant in those army hospitals," the

woman said. "She could easily have caught it there and died. If her husband was missing, it would explain why no one claimed her body to bury her at home."

"Do you have access to old military records for the Civil War period?"

"Sure do." The docent typed in some commands. "Who are you looking for and which side?"

"James and Noah Townsend. Not sure what side they might have fought on. I would think the south, but Mary was from the north. They wouldn't have joined until around January 1862."

After a few more database searches, the older woman shook her head. "Sorry. No record of either name on either side. Not around here during that time frame."

Aury glanced at her watch. "I'm sorry I kept you past closing. This has been so helpful."

"No problem. I love researching history. Please let us know if you find any information to add to our narrative."

"I will. Maybe we'll even transcribe Mary's diaries when we're done, like this website did."

"That would be wonderful. You never know what little tidbit of information will help the next researcher."

Aury thanked her again and left as the door was locked behind her. She couldn't wait to share this letter with Gran and Scott. It felt like they were making small steps forward.

Chapter 41

July 17, 1862

Sarah wrapped the small bundle in an oilskin rag and slipped it into the pocket of her apron. The younger kids still weren't awake, so she had just enough time to get down to the river and back before breakfast.

The silence was refreshing after the storm last night. Emily whimpered late into the night until she finally fell asleep snuggled next to Sarah. The boys arrived at some point, crawling onto the foot of the bed without her noticing until she tried to stretch her legs.

She needed some time to herself to think about how she was going to get information about her mother. She could leave the younger children with Frederick while she walked to the nearest farm, but she wasn't sure how far away that was or how long it would take her. What happened if she didn't return?

The ground was soggy, and the mud sucked at her shoes as she neared the water. As she approached the springhouse, a shot broke the stillness, followed by a few more volleys.

Sarah made a break for the cover of the building. Her foot caught in the mire, and she fell forward. Pushing herself out of the mud, she crawled toward safety. A sharp stab of pain drove her to her belly again. Dragging herself forward by her hands, she made her way to the rocks. Another blow to her back and Sarah went still.

Chapter 42

When they got together on Saturday, Scott handed Aury a folder full of papers and a tattered Bible. "She didn't get very far in her research. Looks like she was just gathering information from family relatives to get started."

"That's something. Gran was saying it might be easier to try to work backward rather than from Mary Townsend forward."

The appraiser arrived, and Scott left Aury reading through the folder while they toured the grounds.

Aury looked over the papers. There were a few computer-printed articles about Eastover, but nothing Aury hadn't already found in her search. A roughly drawn family tree was sketched out on a legal piece of paper. It started with Scott's father Henry Bell and his mother Ellen Spencer.

Henry's side of the tree was fairly stark. He had no siblings. His father, Grant, was the eldest of three brothers and the only one who lived to marry and have a child.

Ellen's side of the family had more details. She had two sisters and two brothers. Those siblings each had two or three children. Aury could understand how much fun Scott and his cousins would have had ranging across Eastover.

Henry must have known the names of his

grandparents—Thomas Jr. and Mary Bell—but not much more than that.

It was a place to start, though. Remembering that she still had the copies of the land deeds she found at the library, she pulled out the backpack she carried which held the documentation she had collected so far.

Rifling through papers, she found the original land grant for 912 acres from the King of England to Henry Brown in 1637. There was another document when a portion of the land was split into parcels for Henry's sons.

She jumped to the most current deed for the 283 acres Scott now owned. Before that, it was in his father's name, and before that, his grandfather Grant Bell who received it as a gift from his father, Matthew Bell Jr. Then she ran across a name she didn't recognize—Marcus Johnson. She made a note to ask Gran if she ran across that name in her genealogy search.

She didn't see any other deeds older than 1955. That meant there was a large gap in the records. She assumed it was because of the war.

Aury jotted in her notebook, not wanting to forget any questions she needed to ask Scott or look up once she got in range of internet service.

Once she had gotten as far as she could with the pages, she carefully opened the Bible. It was obviously well-loved and well-read, judging from the creases in the spine and the spidery handwriting in the margins.

On the opening page where births and deaths were recorded, Scott's great-grandparents were the first listed. Their deaths were recorded as Matthew Bell Jr. in 1971 and Mary in 1973. They had three children. Grant was born in 1935 and died in 1995. He was Scott's grandfather on his dad's side.

Then came Henry, and finally Scott's birth was recorded in 1985. She noted Scott had not updated the dates of his parents' deaths. Was it an oversight or something more?

Putting the Bible aside, she looked over the stack of books Scott had left for her on the picnic table. The three-ring binder held reports for Eastover going back thirty years or more. She was still going through them, furiously scribbling notes, when Scott returned.

"Are you getting hungry yet?"

Aury glanced at her watch, surprised to see it was almost noon. "Time got away from me. How did your meeting with the appraiser go?"

"She said she would run the numbers and call me. I need to send her the insurance claims to show what money I should be getting from them."

"Did she give you any ideas?" Aury asked.

Scott shrugged. "She wasn't very upbeat about the idea. Apparently land like this is only valuable if you sell it to developers. I don't want to do that."

Aury stood. "I brought lunch this time. You're always feeding me." She retrieved a cooler from her car and placed it on the picnic table. "What happens if you can't keep Eastover?"

He sighed. "I always thought I'd watch my kids run through the woods the way I did. Making forts. Searching for buried treasure."

Aury laughed. "You searched for treasure when you were little too?"

"We didn't know it was real at the time or else we would have tried harder." He smiled as he looked around. "This place has so many good memories. Being here the past few weeks has been the most fun I've had in years."

"Even with all the work?"

"Especially with the work. As I said before, seeing a difference in what I do is rewarding. Plus, I enjoy the outdoors much more than living in a city and working in an office."

"Why don't you run this place full time? Move down here?"

"I wish. I still need money to live on. And I have to pay people to help me. Alan's been doing some stuff for me during the week, and that has taken the last of my reserve."

Aury took a bite of her chicken salad, deep in thought.

"Guess we need to work harder to find the buried treasure,"

she said at last.

"Have you given any more thought to following your nose?"

"Actually, yes. Beside a garden, what else would have good smells? I was thinking about drying herbs in a barn."

Scott smacked himself in the forehead. "I'm so stupid. What about food?"

Aury gave him a quizzical look.

"When the house was first built, there was an outdoor kitchen. It was too hot to cook inside, plus it reduced the chance of a house fire."

"But I thought the manor house had a kitchen."

"It did. But there were *two*. One inside for preparation and storage, but another one away from the house."

"Is it still there? I don't remember seeing it."

"The building is long gone, but the old chimney still stands. It's covered in weeds, so you probably didn't notice it."

Aury jumped up. "Let's go."

Scott laughed. "Can I finish my sandwich first?"

"You can take it with you." She tugged on his sleeve, and he gave in. He grabbed the rest of his sandwich and a bottle of water for the ride.

Aury drove the cart while Scott ate.

"How was work this week?" she asked.

"Dull. My mind kept wandering to my next project here."

"What's your next project?" The cart bumped over ruts left by larger work vehicles.

"Well, since the motel isn't livable, I have to think up another way to bring in money. That leaves the manor house and some of the cottages."

"I know this is supposed to be a getaway, but do you think you would do better with internet connection out here? I mean, most people don't want to be disconnected," Aury said.

"I agree. I had the local internet company give me a quote to get service. It runs down the street in front of the drive, so it's just a matter of running the lines to the buildings here. It's doable."

Aury hit a particularly deep hole, and they bounced. "Sorry."

After they parked in front of the manor house, Scott and Aury walked to the left of the building on the side closest to the river. Approaching the overgrown tangle of vines, Aury could make out the elongated stretch of the growth.

"You're right. I never would've noticed this."

Scott pulled the vines away with his hands at the base. The hollow of a brick fireplace became visible, complete with animal droppings and parts of a mouse-sized skeleton.

"But now what?" she said.

"The clue could have been hidden anywhere in the kitchen." They looked around, trying to envision what it would have looked like in Mary's time.

"If it was inside, it wasn't buried," Aury said.

"And if it was hidden inside a box or something, the workers would have noticed when they tore the building down."

"When was that?"

"I'm not sure. We'll have to check your old maps and see if the building is shown."

"But if it was hidden near the fireplace, where would it be? That's all we have to go on."

Scott pulled more ivy away from the bricks. "Old fireplaces had built in niches where you could store things like matches or kindling."

Aury joined in by pulling ivy from the other side. She ran her hands up the brick surface, feeling for any sign of looseness.

"Here!" Scott held a rough brick in his hand. Aury started to reach into the opening, but Scott stopped her. "Wait. Let's look first. Who knows what spiders may have taken up residence."

Aury shuddered and waited while he pulled out his cell phone and set it to flashlight mode. After poking inside the hole with a stick a few times, he fished out a tin box.

He handed it to Aury and shut off the light.

Gently she opened the lid. It was full of matchsticks. Her shoulders drooped. "Guess it was too good to be true."

"Don't give up so quickly."

She handed him the box as she turned to search the fireplace again.

Scott didn't get a firm hold on the tin, and it slipped from his fingers. The sticks scattered across the grass. As they knelt to put them back in the box, Scott started laughing.

"What's up?" Aury asked.

He reached into the tin and pried a folded piece of paper from the bottom. "Three guesses as to what this is."

Aury grinned. "Where do we go next?"

Chapter 43

July 17, 1862

S arah? Where are you? Emily has been crying for you."
Frederick broke through the trees. Seeing his sister's
muddy figure on the ground by the springhouse, he
laughed out loud. "Wait until Thomas sees you! You will never
be able to call him filthy again."

When Sarah didn't move, Frederick ventured closer.
"Sarah?" A note of panic rose in his throat. He swallowed hard
and forced himself to get closer. He looked around frantically,
searching for the reason his sister wasn't responding. He knelt
by her side and placed his hand on her shoulder. He shook
gently, hoping she would awaken. A small cry escaped his lips
when he moved her hair away from her face and saw her dead
eyes.

He scrambled, crablike, away from the body. Now he could
see a dark spot on Sarah's dress that wasn't mud. He heard
movement in the trees behind him.

"Frederick? Sarah? Come on already. I'm hungry, and
Emily is crying again." Thomas's voice rang out in the morning
air.

Frederick jumped to his feet and ran for the path to the
woods. "I'm coming. Let's go find food."

"Where's Sarah?"

"She'll be along eventually. You know how she is." Frederick put one arm around his brother while wiping tears from his eyes with the other hand.

Chapter 44

Present Day

"For where your treasure is, there your heart will be also," Scott read.

"Doesn't sound too helpful. We don't know where the treasure is. That's the problem," Aury said.

"Isn't that a Bible verse?"

"Sounds like it. I've heard it before somewhere."

"I have the family Bible at the cottage," Scott said.

"Let's look in the manor house. I want to see if Mary's family Bible was there anyway. Yours starts with your great-grandparents."

They walked into the house and straight to the library. Aury searched from left to right while Scott went right to left.

"Scott, I think I found it. Can you reach it? It's on the second shelf."

He pulled down the book. It was definitely an old Bible. Aury sat on the couch as she opened the red leather cover.

The front page listed the marriage of James and Mary on September 9, 1846. Under that, the births of seven children were listed, two included the date of death as well. No other entries had been made.

Aury felt drawn to this book as she had Mary's diaries.

Something about reading a woman's handwriting from the 1800s brought history to life for her.

The book was printed in Philadelphia in 1827 by the American Bible Society. The thin paper contained scribbles in the margins. She turned to the end.

"No index," she said. "We'll have to try a more modern Bible. Do you mind if I take this with me? I'd like to see if I can read Mary's notes."

"Of course you can take it. How do you know it's Mary's handwriting and not James?"

She gave him a condescending look. "Really? Who do you think was more likely to write in the Bible? The educated mother of five who was homeschooling, or the farmer husband who spent most of his time outdoors?"

Scott shrugged.

"Actually, I recognize her handwriting from the diaries," she admitted. She looked closer at the scribble. "Can I see the clue again?"

Scott handed her the slip of paper.

Aury looked between the paper and the book. "The handwriting doesn't match."

"So?"

"It might not mean anything, but I don't think Mary wrote this note."

"No way we'd have two different treasure hunts going on at once," Scott said.

"I agree. But remember the note we found in the book? Sarah might have taken over where her mother left off."

"Does that change anything in our search?"

"I don't know. Maybe not. But we should check the handwriting."

Scott looked at his watch. "Let's head back. I need to get some things done. You can check the Bible at my place."

She continued thumbing through the pages as Scott drove the utility cart. At the cottage, Scott jumped out. "I need to gather some things, then I could use some help. Are you up for it?"

"Definitely." Aury placed the Bible with the other papers in her car. While she waited, she looked at the later version of Scott's family Bible. The index under treasure told her to look under money. A quick scan there didn't reveal any obvious clues.

"Let's go," Scott said.

Aury set the book aside and joined him.

They drove to the clearing which held the small cottages they had raided for food during their stay in the manor house.

"I see you got the tree off the roof," Aury said.

"The tree service took care of it at the same time they cleared your cars. That industry makes out after a storm."

"How bad is the damage?"

"Surprisingly, not bad." He pointed to a spot on the right side. "The wood structure wasn't broken, but I have to replace those shingles. That's where you come in."

Aury smiled. "Great. You're using me for my brawn."

"You can handle it. Besides, I prefer to have someone here if I'm going to be climbing on roofs."

Once Scott ascended the ladder with a bundle of shingles, Aury handed him a rope attached at the other end to a bucket of roofing nails. She watched as he raised the contents.

"Pretty fancy," she said.

"Laziness breeds invention, or something like that. I didn't want to have to keep climbing up and down the ladder."

While he set to work, Aury walked through the cottages, making a list of repairs to be completed to prepare the rooms for rent.

When she finished, she wandered around the clearing, taking note of any work needing to be done. There was a firepit to clean out, so she went in search of a rake.

As she finished clearing debris away from the pit, she heard a loud crash.

"Sorry!" Scott called from his spot on the roof. "I should have warned you. I'm done up here and didn't feel like carrying the extra shingles down."

Aury put her hand over her heart. "You scared the crap out of me."

"Me too, honestly. I didn't realize it would be so loud." He lowered the bucket then descended the ladder. Grabbing a water from the utility cart, he looked over the notes Aury had taken.

"With the road fixed and the electricity back on, I can open for business again—at least for the cottages. Housekeeping will need to clean and air them out," Scott said.

"That should get you some money for the other repairs."

Scott tossed the list into the utility cart. Resting against the vehicle, he crossed his arms over his chest. "I've been thinking about the clue. We don't know where the treasure is, but can we figure out where the heart is?"

Aury thought about it. "There's another saying, home is where the heart is. Could we be talking about the house again?"

"Not specific enough. To say she hid the treasure in the house isn't much of a clue. Besides, if Sarah's goal was to hide it from visitors, inside doesn't make sense."

"The hearth of the detached kitchen doesn't make sense for the same reason."

"This is one for your grandmother. Can you ask her what she thinks?"

"I'm sure she'll be happy to help."

Chapter 45

After feeding both kids and putting Emily down for a nap, Frederick searched for a way to occupy Thomas. Sending him searching for a beehive away from the river may work.

"Where's Sarah? She shouldn't have missed lunch," Thomas said.

Frederick was struggling to keep it together. He didn't know how or if he should tell Thomas about Sarah, but he also didn't know how he could keep it a secret. He would have to bury her, and he wasn't sure if he could handle that task alone. He had no idea how to reach his mother or when she might be home. She had already been gone too long.

"Frederick, what is your problem? You're acting strange."

"Thomas, I have something to tell you, but you can't let Emily find out."

Thomas looked at him suspiciously. "Are you trying to get me in trouble?"

"Let's go out to the porch." Frederick steered his brother to sit on the step. Once he was sure they were out of earshot, he took a deep breath to steady his nerves and began.

"Sarah's been hurt."

Thomas jumped to his feet. "Where is she? Let's go help her."

Frederick pulled him down. "She can't be helped. She was hurt very badly."

Thomas stared at him and water formed in his eyes. That's all it took for the tears to overtake Frederick. Through sniffles, Frederick told Thomas about finding Sarah by the river.

"Are you sure she's dead?" Thomas asked. "We need to go check again. You shouldn't have left her alone."

"I'm sure." Frederick rested his head in his hands. "We need to do something with her. We can't leave her there. She needs to be buried."

Thomas stood and took his brother's hand. "Let's get this done before Emily wakes up."

Frederick smiled weakly at Thomas, thankful he was acting so bravely. "Let's get the shovels."

The boys carried their shovels down the path toward the water. The closer they got, the slower they walked. Neither were in a hurry to see their sister's lifeless body.

Chapter 46

That quote is from Matthew," Gran said when Aury read her the clue. She picked up a well-worn Bible from the coffee table near where she sat in the morning to read. Flipping the pages, she skimmed quickly.

It was a beautiful Sunday afternoon, and the women had finished their lunch after church. Now they were relaxing and drinking iced tea at Gran's house.

"Here it is. Matthew six, verse twenty-one. But if you start at first twenty, it says, 'But store up for yourselves treasures in heaven, where moth and rust do not destroy, and where thieves do not break in and steal. For where your treasure is, there your heart will be also.'"

"Okay, don't laugh at me, but I think I read that in a Harry Potter book," Aury said.

Gran gave her a strange look.

"It was written on Dumbledore's sister's tombstone."

"Well, I doubt a clue from the eighteen-hundreds was referencing the writings of J. K. Rowling," Gran said.

Smiling, Aury was pleased her grandmother was keeping up with popular titles. Suddenly Aury sat straight in her chair.

"What is it?" Gran asked.

"What if the idea is the same though?"

"What are you talking about?"

"Dumbledore's heart was with his sister. She was his treasure."

"Didn't you say some of Mary's children didn't live?"

"Two died young," Aury confirmed.

"Is there a graveyard on the property?" Gran said.

"Not that I've seen, but I'll ask Scott."

"That poor boy. He has his hands full." Gran picked up her knitting needles, her hands moving in precise movements as she worked the yarn. "I don't know how he's going to get Eastover back in working order while living in northern Virginia."

"He has Alan to help."

"He needs to hire a few more people. His parents didn't do him any favors letting it get so run down."

"They had other things on their mind."

"I guess there could be people buried anywhere, as we saw with the skeleton by the river," Scott said when Aury asked him during their phone conversation later that night. "I've never seen a graveyard on the property. I wouldn't even know where to begin looking."

"Graveyards are often by churches. There were some old photo albums in the manor house. One picture had a building like a church or a chapel. Is there a church there?"

"No. You've seen all the buildings that are left."

"What about the haunted woods?" Aury asked.

"What about them?"

"Why were they haunted?"

"My grandparents never told us."

"Graveyards are often said to be haunted."

"This is when I need to remind you ghosts aren't real." Scott chuckled.

"I know that! But the stories came from somewhere. Do you remember where the haunted woods were?"

"Of course, but I'm not going there after dark."

"Ha, ha," Aury said. "I'll protect you, you big scaredy cat."

Chapter 47

Sept 12, 1862

Frederick tried his best to smile and be patient like his big sister, but he was struggling to come up with food for dinner.

He reached into the cupboard for the last jar of pickles. They had flour but he had no idea how to make bread. He searched another shelf and found a bag of dried apples. That wasn't going to be enough.

"Thomas, I need you to go check the oyster traps," Frederick said.

Thomas's eyes grew wide in alarm.

"You don't need to go by the springhouse. Check farther downstream. Be quick. There's a storm coming. Bring the shells to the house, and I'll show you how to open them."

At that, Thomas grew excited. This was a chore typically reserved for the oldest children. He grabbed a bucket and rushed off.

Emily tottered in from the dining room looking for Sarah. It had been over a month since the boys buried their sister, but Emily didn't understand that Sarah wasn't coming back.

The thought of her alone in the cold, wet ground brought tears to his eyes. He pushed the thought aside and reached down to pick up his baby sister.

"Let's go see what's in the garden."

Frederick split his time between picking whatever looked close to ripe while trying to keep Emily from eating things she shouldn't. There was very little left in the garden now, and he wasn't sure when the next vegetables would be ready.

"Run!"

Frederick jumped at the sound of his brother's voice.

Thomas's little legs pumped furiously while the pail smacked against his knees. "Run!" he yelled again.

Frederick grabbed Emily and followed Thomas into the house.

"What's going on?" Frederick asked.

"They saw me. I didn't mean to let them. I was digging, and then they were there. I'm sorry. I didn't mean to."

Frederick placed his hand on his brother's head. "Calm down, right now!" When Thomas stopped jumping around, Frederick went on. "Who saw you?"

"Three men. I don't know who they are. They're coming. I saw them by the river."

Frederick looked out the window toward the river. "Were they in uniform?"

"I don't think so. They had on big hats. Their skin was like Auntie Dee's."

"They were colored? Are you sure? Was there a white man with them?"

"No, just three dark ones. What are we going to do?"

Frederick looked around nervously. "Hide."

Chapter 48

Present Day

I'm thinking about giving my two weeks' notice," Scott said.

Aury stopped walking, caught by surprise. "What? I thought you liked your job."

"I do, but I like this more. I have had so much fun working outside and making decisions for myself." He took her arm to get her moving again. "The scrub you did on my accounting books was an eye-opener. I wish my father had someone like you to watch over the numbers. I think he lost track of things when Mom got sick."

Aury's audit had pointed out a few cost-saving measures for the business, as well as determining the prices Scott was charging for rentals was far below market value.

As they walked under the shade of the trees toward the clearing, Aury struggled with questions.

"Not to be a stick in the mud, and you can tell me it's none of my business, but won't you be taking a huge pay cut?"

"The insurance came through; that will help with most of the repairs, especially because I'm doing a lot of the work myself. The lease is up on my apartment soon, and that will save a pretty penny every month. Northern Virginia is ridiculously expensive. I can live in the cottage for now."

"Maybe you can apply for the property to be put on the National Historic Record," Aury suggested.

"How will that help me?"

"You may be eligible for state or federal tax credits. If you qualify for both, you could save a lot on fixing things up."

"Super idea. I'll look into it." Scott had a huge smile.

"You do look happy," Aury said.

"I am. Lately I feel like I've been torn between two worlds. Maybe I need to take the leap."

"And when we find the treasure, you'll be rich."

"There is that," he agreed. "But until then, I'll keep a close eye on my books and eat like a college student."

They arrived at the clearing and were met by Alan.

"So good to see you again," Aury said to him.

"I hear you've been helping out a lot around here. Thanks for keeping Scott motivated."

"How did your property fare? Did you have any problems?"

"No. My place was fine. I had to help my mother, though. No one hurt. Just a lot to tidy up." Alan gestured toward the cottages. "The cleaners came by, and these are ready to go."

"Good thing. Two of them are rented for next weekend already," Scott said.

"That's wonderful news!" Aury said.

"Things are picking up."

"I went by the dining hall earlier. I'm glad you threw away the food, but I needed to scrub everything out," Alan said. "I assume the renters this weekend won't need any food prepared."

"No, they'll take care of themselves. Until I can rent the manor house, I don't think we'll have any large groups."

"What about campers?" Aury asked.

Both men looked at her.

"You have the space. Why don't you open up some spots for tent camping? You may get some scout troops interested. Or church groups."

"That's an interesting idea. We can look at the area behind the dining hall. It's fairly flat with shade, and the campers can use the restrooms in the halls." Scott was excited.

"Do you have to provide a place for a shower?" she asked.

"I think we can rig an outdoor shower. We can run a hose from the dining hall and set up some wooden stalls for privacy," Alan said.

Aury shivered. "Are you kidding? That'll be way too cold this time of the year. Is there any room inside?"

Without another word, they started walking toward the dining hall to check the options.

"What are you going to do about the motel?" Alan asked.

A long sigh escaped Scott's lips. "There's no saving it. The fire department cleared me to go inside to see what I can salvage, but they want me to wear a hard hat."

"We should do it before the next rain if we want to save anything," Alan suggested.

"Aury, would you like to go with us and see if there's anything left belonging to your friends?"

"Sure. I came ready to work."

"I thought you'd say that." Smiling, he placed a hard hat on her head.

Hours later, they had cleared out everything of value. Scott and Alan decided it wasn't worth trying to recover the appliances in the small kitchen. They would buy new when the time came. Same with the washers and dryers.

The bedding from the rooms where the roof wasn't damaged was packed into the back of Alan's truck so he could take it to town and have it cleaned. The rest they left for the dumpster.

The quilting supplies had been mostly cleared away before the ladies reclaimed their cars. What was left wasn't worth saving. Aury took notes on what she threw out to make it easier for the ladies to file insurance claims if they wanted to.

Alan waved goodbye as he left Aury and Scott drinking from

their water bottles in front of the broken-down motel.

"I forgot to tell you; Dr. Vinson called me yesterday and asked if we can come by," Scott said. "She's dating the skeleton to the 1860s. Said it fits with what they found with the bones, as well as the Minié ball and photograph found with them."

"Makes sense. I still wonder why she was buried there."

"We'll never know."

The cicadas and frogs sounded in the silence as Aury and Scott got lost in their own musings.

Aury started when a thought hit her. "Is that where the haunted woods are? By the river? Maybe she was haunting them."

Scott's burst of laughter at her excitement sent the water he was drinking shooting from his mouth. He wiped the wetness from his chin as he continued to laugh.

"You're really excited about ghost hunting, aren't you?"

Aury looked sheepish. "A little. I was the strange child who enjoyed ghost tours through old towns when we were on vacation. I think the history is fascinating."

"Sorry, but no. The haunted woods are across the property to the east a bit. There are no buildings over there, so I don't usually have a reason to go over that way. We can check it out after we grab some food."

As they leaned against the car drinking, a work truck pulled in.

A short, stocky man stepped out carrying a clipboard. "Mr. Bell?"

"That's me." Scott offered his hand.

"I'm here about your demolition work. Is this the only building?"

"Thankfully, yes. Any idea when you can get started?"

"It's next on the list. I need to check with the utility companies to make sure everything has been shut off. We'll start next week."

Aury wandered away, leaving the men to discuss details of the work to be done.

Chapter 49

Sept 12, 1862

Emily started whining. Hoping to appease her, Frederick
handed her another piece of dried fruit.

"I'm tired of sitting here," Thomas complained, not for
the first time.

"We'll go inside soon," Frederick said.

"You said that hours ago. I'm getting eaten alive." Thomas
swatted at something on his leg.

Frederick was conflicted. He knew they couldn't stay out
here all night, but he was worried about anyone who might be
watching the house. He hadn't seen any movement. "Just a few
more minutes. It's almost full dark."

With the last piece of fruit eaten, Emily began to fuss again.
Frederick couldn't keep her quiet any longer. He stood, trying
to work the kinks out of his legs from staying still so long. "All
right. Let's go."

Hand in hand, the three worked their way toward the house.

"I need to stop at the privy," Thomas said.

"Can't it wait?"

"I've been waiting for hours. And this isn't something I can
take care of in the woods."

Frederick sighed. "Go, but hurry. Come in through the

kitchen door." He picked up Emily and dashed to the house.

Thomas fastened his britches and stepped out of the privy, very much relieved. He closed the door quietly so it wouldn't slam. He only made it three steps when a strong hand clamped over his mouth.

Kicking and thrashing, he fought against the arm wrapped around his small chest. A second set of hands captured his ankles, and they carried him back into the woods.

"Quiet down now. We don't plan on hurting you," the deep voice told him.

Thomas could only make out the whites of two sets of eyes in the deep dark of the trees. He gave up struggling for now. He wondered if he could outrun them when given the chance.

"I'm going to uncover your mouth. Don't yell or I might have to do something to quiet you."

The pressure was released, and Thomas took in a gulp of air.

"How many people in the house?" This time it was a different voice, still deep but raspy.

Thomas stared without speaking.

"We ain't gonna hurt you. We be looking for your parents."

"They aren't here," he blurted out. Maybe they would move on.

"When they coming back?"

Tears came unbidden to Thomas's eyes.

The man must have noticed because he turned to whisper to someone behind him.

The deep voice who had been holding him asked, "Which side of the fight is your pa on?"

Thomas didn't understand the question. His dad had gone to town to buy livestock and never came home. He wasn't fighting anyone.

"Where's your ma?"

No reply.

"Randolph, I told you, these kids ain't got parents here," came the raspy voice.

"Is it just the three of you?" the man called Randolph asked Thomas.

Thomas held silent.

"C'mon, boy. We don't have time for this. We need to move."

Thinking if he gave them what they were looking for, they might leave, he finally gave in. "It's just my brother, my little sister, and me. Our parents went to town and never came home. We don't have anything you'd want. We barely have anything for ourselves."

"How long ago did they leave?"

Thomas shrugged. "Months. Early summer, I think."

The men shared a look. "Samuel, keep hold of him. Zack, you go on ahead and listen by the door. Let's go meet his family," Randolph said.

Samuel took Thomas by the upper arm as they walked out of the tree line. "No sound, or someone might end up hurt," he told Thomas.

Crossing the lawn, Thomas tried to think of a way to warn his brother. A squeeze on his arm reminded him what these men were capable of.

Randolph pulled open the kitchen door.

"What took you so long?" Frederick said, coming down the stairs. "Emily's in bed but she's asking for you."

Frederick froze in the doorway to the kitchen as he took in the two men flanking his brother.

"I'm sorry," Thomas whispered.

Chapter 50

Present Day

Entering the canopy of trees provided instant relief from the scorching heat. No discernible path presented itself, so Aury and Scott picked their way over fallen trees and waved away the cobwebs.

As Aury tried to wipe a particularly sticky web from her arm, she said, "This part of the woods doesn't look any different from anything else I've seen. Why was it haunted?"

"Don't know. Maybe because it was the farthest away from the house."

The branches overhead blocked out a view of the sky, and the sound of small animals scurrying through the underbrush was loud in the silence.

"There's a clearing around here somewhere," Scott said. "This way, I think." He adjusted course and Aury followed.

Sunlight acted as a spotlight to illuminate the tall grass in the center of the woods.

"This can't be a natural clearing," Aury said. "It's too circular."

She cut across the center and approached a huge mound of kudzu. "I can't stand this stuff. It takes over and smothers the other plants and trees." She pulled at the hardy vine.

"It's kind of creepy how it covers things and takes on their shape," Scott noted.

Aury laughed. "Maybe that's what haunted you."

"Could be. From here, it looks like a ghost holding out his arms to grab you."

She looked up. Taking a few more steps away, she stared intently at the mound that had attracted her attention.

"I think there's something under all that," she said.

"Of course there is. More trees and bushes."

"No, it looks too square." She got closer and tried to create a hole in the center of the mass with her hands.

"We need something to cut with," Scott said.

"Let's get some tools. I think I see rock or stone." Aury's excitement was contagious.

"Another mystery?"

"Everything's a mystery until we answer the questions."

They hiked to where the utility cart was parked. Scott grabbed the hedge trimmers and handed Aury the long-handled pruning shears.

As they approached the clearing again, Aury pointed to the right of the largest kudzu mound. "See where it dips down there? Could that be a path?"

Scott looked at the vegetation. "Could be. I don't know where it would go, but there are no trees there. Looks deliberate."

Aury resumed her spot in the middle of the mound and cut away at the vines. Scott joined her, slicing and snipping the only sound for the next thirty minutes.

"Yes! I was right!" Aury pulled aside the last of the loose vines to reveal a wall of stone.

"Definitely manmade. We can't unbury it with these tools. We need something more robust. I wonder what would kill this stuff."

"We could ask the master gardeners. They've been helpful so far."

"Let's do that. In the meantime, want to check out the potential path?"

"Absolutely." Aury put the shears over her shoulder and walked toward the break in the circle.

"It does look like the trees were cleared, but it isn't very wide."

"Well, if it was made years ago, these trees lining the path have grown larger, making the opening narrower."

"It has to be old if I don't remember it. It certainly wasn't built for cars. Maybe buggies?"

They walked along the winding path until they were joined by a trickling stream running along their route. "I don't remember this either," Scott said.

Following the stream, they walked until the woods started to thin out. A rumbling sounded in the distance.

"It's not supposed to storm today," Aury said.

Scott cocked his head. "I don't think that's thunder."

They came around another bend in the path as a truck rolled across a wooden bridge over the stream.

"I know where we are now," Scott said. "The entrance to Eastover is that way." He pointed off to his right. "I never knew there was another entrance. I wonder why."

"To get to whatever is buried back there, I'd guess."

Scott glanced at the sky. "We better get going. We don't want to get stuck in the woods in the dark."

"Afraid of the ghosts?"

Chapter 51

Sept 12, 1862

The three black men and two boys sat at the dining room table as if this were a common occurrence. Frederick had brought out a few yams he had boiled, and the men had finished them off. When the boys learned the men were escaped slaves from the fields of North Carolina and not soldiers here to steal their food, they relaxed their guard a bit.

"You can't stay here alone," Randolph told the boys. "What will you do when winter comes? You said you're already low on supplies."

"If Mother doesn't find us when she comes home, she'll be mad," Thomas said.

"Sorry, son. I don't think your ma's coming back. Something happened for her to be away this long," Zack said gently.

Thomas looked at Frederick who gave a slow nod in agreement.

"Where will we go?" Thomas asked.

"Where's your kin?" Samuel said.

"Our grandparents live in Pennsylvania," said Frederick.

"We're heading toward the Union troops to join the fight. Maybe they can get you to Pennsylvania," Zack suggested.

"The Army don't have time for no kids," Samuel said.

"They'd be put in some orphan home."

Randolph mulled it over. "I reckon we could get them to their family."

Four sets of eyes looked at him in disbelief. "And how do you suppose that's going to happen?" Zack said.

"What if we had passes? Can you write?" Samuel asked Frederick.

"Sure. If you tell me what to say."

"Does your daddy have any papers lying around? We might be able to figure it out."

"What are you thinking?" Zack said.

"What if we here were tasked by our master to take these young'uns north to see their family. Who would stop us?" Samuel said.

"Just any slave catcher in the area, that's who," Randolph said.

"If we stayed in the shadows of the Union troops much as possible, they would protect us without knowing it."

The group was silent as they thought through the plan.

"Do we have to walk?" Thomas asked. "Emily won't be able to go fast."

"You got horses? Or mules?" Zack asked.

"Dad and Noah took the horses and wagon when they left. We have the pony wagon. We could put Emily in there," Frederick said.

"We can't leave Betsy," Thomas said.

"Who's Betsy? I thought it was only you three," Samuel said.

"Betsy's the goat. We can tie her to the wagon. It'll be good for Emily to have milk along the way," Frederick explained.

Randolph stood. "We should get on the road as soon as possible. Let's sleep tonight. We'll gather what we can tomorrow and leave when it's dark again."

Thomas's eyes started to well up again. Placing a reassuring hand on his shoulder, Randolph added, "You can leave your ma a note telling her where you're going so she don't worry."

Chapter 52

Present Day

The sky was overcast as Aury and Scott made their way through the trees to the clearing.

"I sprayed weed killer at the base of the mound last week before I went to work, but I don't think it made a dent," Scott told her.

"The master gardeners said it would take multiple applications before there was a chance of anything killing this stuff. It's best to get it in the winter."

"I don't want to wait that long. Do you?"

"No way. It's something amazing. I can feel it."

Scott held up the chainsaw he was carrying. "It might be a little overkill, but it will be faster than attacking it by hand."

Pulling her gloves on as they stepped into the slightly brighter spot that revealed the clearing, Aury said, "It'll almost be sad when we find the treasure."

"What?"

"I mean, it'll be fun, but then we won't have anything to look forward to anymore," she explained.

"I'll look forward to not going to work in an office every day." He examined the kudzu, determining the best place to start. "But, honestly, what are the chances we'll discover something valuable?"

Aury shrugged. "What they considered valuable then and what we consider valuable today may be very different things. You shouldn't get your hopes up."

"You're one to talk."

They set to work at the base of the plant, Aury tugging the vines tight while Scott easily cut through them with the chainsaw. Soon they had sliced a twelve-foot swath and started working across five foot higher and parallel to the ground.

When the buzz of the chainsaw stopped, the silence was deafening. They had scared all the animals away, and even the bugs were holding back their din.

Scott pushed his safety glasses to the top of his head. Aury wiped the sweat from her face with the sleeve of her shirt.

"Ready to see what's under here?" he asked.

Together, they pulled and tugged at the vines until a wall of green-covered stone loomed in front of them. A single, cracked pane of glass dark with dirt centered the opening. Aury approached the window and rubbed away some of the grime with her gloved hand. The bottom lip was five feet above the ground, allowing Aury to peer in at the dark interior.

Scott tugged the vines to the left of where Aury was standing. "I think there's another window here."

Exchanging the chainsaw for the long-handled pruning shears they brought with them, Scott trimmed carefully around the glass. "This is stained glass."

"I'll bet it's the church from the photo album!" Aury said.

Scott peered through the filthy window. "It's going to take a lot of pruning to get inside this building."

"Now we need to find the graveyard."

"What graveyard?"

"If there was a graveyard on the property, wouldn't it make sense to be next to the church?"

Scott looked around. "Well, it isn't in the clearing or along the path. It's either on the other side of this building or under that mess." He gestured toward the uneven line of kudzu forming hills and tall, human-shaped piles to the left of the building.

"We can narrow it down. They wouldn't have buried anything right next to the trees."

"If they used grave markers at all, they might have been wooden, and there won't be any trace left," Scott said.

Aury's face dropped in disappointment. "I didn't think about that."

"Let's see if we can make our way to the other side of the building."

Taking a wide berth around the thickest part of the kudzu, they walked down the potential path a short distance before cutting into the woods. After stomping and trampling through the brush, they came to another, though smaller, clearing. Kudzu was in evidence here as well, but it grew lower to the ground, looking like waves of green.

"This has got to be it!" Aury exclaimed.

"I don't know where to begin," Scott said.

Aury jumped in like a child chasing the sea. She lifted her knees high to keep her feet from tangling in the vines.

"I don't think you'll find anything like that. We need to be more systematic about it," Scott said. "Let's take a break and come back later. I need to check on the guests."

Disappointed, Aury climbed out of the mess. "I don't want to wait until winter to locate the treasure."

"I'll do some research to see if something else can be done. I don't want to wait either, but it's been hidden this long. A little while longer won't matter."

Chapter 53

Sept 13, 1862

Y ou better carry the papers," Randolph told Frederick.
Frederick tucked them into a pocket of his pants. He
placed a bundle containing the last of their food stores
in the pony wagon next to Emily, who immediately attempted
to crawl over the side.

"Here, take your baby," he said, putting her into the wagon
again. The tattered doll Mother had sewn for her only two years
earlier proved to be a sufficient distraction, and he was glad he'd
remembered to bring it.

Samuel took his place at the front of the wagon and lifted
the wooden handles meant to attach to a pony harness. Thomas
ran in from the rear of the house, leading Betsy by a rope.

"I fed her again and gave her water," he said.

"What's hanging on her?" Zack asked.

Thomas adjusted the net bags resting across Betsy's back
and down her sides. "Just some stuff we might need. She can
carry them for a little while. They aren't heavy."

He glanced toward the barn. "Who's going to feed the
chickens?"

Frederick, with a look of guilty knowledge, glanced at the
men—Randolph had prepped some of the birds to eat along the

way. "I tossed out extra feed."

Randolph added, "They'll be able to fend for themselves. They eat bugs."

"Let's move out," Samuel said as he tugged the wagon to get it started. The other two men walked behind it while the boys flanked their sister on either side.

Emily clapped her hands and giggled at the unexpected wagon ride.

"If anyone asks, we're traveling at night because it's cooler and easier on your sister so she can sleep," Randolph reminded the boys.

"What are you going to say if they ask about your parents?" Zack quizzed Thomas.

"Pa's away in the fighting. Ma died when Emily was born."

Zack turned to Frederick. "And where are we headed?"

"Pa told you to take us to our grandparents in Philadelphia. Said he'd come for us there."

"Do you think he'll really come?" Thomas asked.

Frederick shrugged. He didn't want to think about his parents. He was more concerned with keeping his siblings safe. He was taking a big chance with these three men, but he figured if they were going to do them harm, they would have done it by now.

Chapter 54

Present Day

T he results of the DNA are in. The skeleton shares some of
your same markers," Dr. Vinson said to Scott and Aury
when they walked in her lab at the college.

"So what does that mean?" Scott asked.

"You are most likely related to the person who was buried
on your property. It wasn't a stranger passing by. Any idea who
it might be?"

Aury jumped in. "You said it was a female from the Civil
War timeframe, right? It could be Mary who wrote in the diaries
or one of her daughters. She had two."

"But didn't you say the younger sister was born in 1860?
She still would have been a toddler during the war." Scott did
the math in his head. "The chance of a gunshot wound from a
Minié ball in 1875 or so, is not likely."

"That leaves Mary or Sarah, the older daughter," Aury said.

"We can narrow it down even further," Dr. Vinson said.
"This woman never gave birth, so it rules out Mary."

"How can you tell that from a skeleton?" Scott asked.

"If she had given birth, we would see small pockmarks
along the inside of the pelvic bone caused by the tearing of the
ligaments during childbirth." Dr. Vinson held up the pelvic bone

and pointed at the area. "As you can see, this is clear."

Aury looked at Scott. "Then it's probably Sarah. I'm glad she has a name. It feels wrong to keep thinking of her as the skeleton."

"We appreciate you letting us run these tests for you. It's been a great project for the graduate students," Dr. Vinson said. She handed him the picture frame wrapped gently with tissue paper.

Thanking her, he opened the package. "It's beautiful! You did a wonderful job cleaning it up."

"It was the students. I only offered advice."

He tucked the paper around the frame again. "Thanks again for meeting us on a Sunday. It's getting harder for me to take time off work during the week."

"No problem. I had some prepping to do for classes next week anyway," Dr. Vinson said.

"If it's okay, I'd like to get the bones when you're finished."

Aury gave Scott a curious look.

"I think it would be nice to bury her in the cemetery by the old church. It's the least we can do."

Aury put a hand on his arm. "I think that's perfect."

Dr. Vinson assured him she would make the necessary arrangements. They said their goodbyes and walked out of the building.

"Now what?" Scott asked.

"Let's go see Gran. She said she found something for you."

The smell of fresh baking filled their nostrils as they climbed the steps to the kitchen door.

"What smells so wonderful?" Scott asked as Aury hugged her grandmother.

"Nothing's better than warm bread and honey to keep the energy up," Gran said. "Would you like tea?"

Both accepted and Gran bustled around the kitchen. Aury took in the stacks of papers on the table. "What's all this?"

"I was working my way through the genealogy. I figured if Scott's great-grandfather Matthew Junior was born in 1913, he most likely served in World War II. There are quite a few online databases that capture information about soldiers."

"When did you get so handy with the computer?" Aury asked.

Gran smiled. "The young man at the library was most helpful. I bribed him with cookies."

"That would work for me." Scott grinned.

Gran handed them each a cup and a plate with a thick slab of bread and honey, then cleared a spot at the table for them to sit.

"Matthew was in the war, along with his two brothers. Sadly, his brothers were killed in action. From their death notification paperwork the Army had, I was able to get the names of their parents—Matthew Bell Senior and Pearl Johnson Bell from Bel Air, Maryland."

Gran handed Scott a piece of paper. "Matthew Senior died in World War I, leaving Pearl alone with the three boys. The Army's records of pension show Pearl moving to Doylestown, Pennsylvania. I thought about where I would go if I was widowed with three children to raise."

"Your parents," Aury and Scott said together. They exchanged a look and laughed.

"Right." Gran searched through more papers until she found what she was looking for. "The address she moved to was owned by Henry and Victoria Johnson. Want to take a guess what Victoria's maiden name was?"

They shook their heads.

"Townsend!" Gran declared.

"You tracked Scott's family to the Townsends? Related to the Mary Townsend from the diary? That's incredible," Aury said, beaming.

"I can't believe you've done all this work for me. You're the greatest," Scott said.

Waving her hand, Gran brushed aside his comments. "This was good exercise for my brain. I may need to do some research into our family lines next."

"So Pearl was Victoria's daughter but how was Victoria related to Mary?" Aury asked.

"Those records are still a little sketchy, but I'm working on it. Looking at the average age of when people married and had kids back then, I'd guess there's a generation between Mary's kids and Victoria. Since her last name is Townsend, we'd assume Victoria is a descendent of one of the boys—Frederick or Thomas."

"That reminds me. When I checked the deed records, I found the name Marcus Johnson. Have you run across him anywhere?" Aury asked.

"No, but I wasn't looking." She took a note on the inside of the folder.

Gran gathered the papers into a pile and tapped them neatly into a stack. "I'll call the Doylestown library tomorrow and see if they can help me with family records from the 1800s. I might be able to fill in the missing piece."

"Can you remind me again why this is important?" Scott asked.

"It may not be," Aury admitted. "But maybe if we can find more of your family, they can fill in some missing information about the skeleton—I mean Sarah—and the treasure. Maybe someone already found it, and we're wasting our time looking for it."

"Are you having fun?" Gran asked.

They looked at her curiously.

"It can't be a waste of time if you are enjoying the search. And look at everything you learned about your past and each other," Gran said.

Aury felt the heat rise in her cheeks and took a quick bite of bread.

Chapter 55

Back at Eastover, Aury went directly to the library in the manor house. She flipped through the photo albums until she found the picture of the couple standing in front of a stone building.

She pulled out the strong magnifying glass she had borrowed from Gran. "Yes!"

Scott rushed into the room. "What?"

"Check out this picture." She thrust the album and magnifying glass into his hands. She pointed with excitement. "What do you see?"

He concentrated for a minute. "It looks like it could be the building we found. The stones look right."

"Look *beside* the building," she emphasized.

He took a closer look. His head snapped up and he met her eyes. "Are those white stones?"

"Looks like it to me. They aren't shaped like traditional headstones, but that doesn't mean they weren't used as markers."

"So that tells us the graveyard is somewhere under that mess of kudzu." He looked at the photo again. "We can use the height of the building and people standing in front to approximate where those stones are in relation to the building."

Aury pointed at something in the picture. "That looks like a front door, so not the area where we were cutting. It has to be around the other side."

"What are we waiting for?"

"Don't you have guests?" Aury asked.

Scott looked at his watch. "Okay. Let's go by and see if they have everything they need. I can pick up a few things from my cabin."

After a quick stop to determine all was well with the paying visitors, Aury and Scott were soon loading a backpack with a few essential items.

This time, Scott drove the utility cart out of the front entrance to Eastover and down the main road. Traffic was never heavy this far into Surry County, but they hugged the side of the road anyway. As they approached the wooden bridge, Scott slowed and steered onto a barely visible path.

It was bumpier than usual, and at times, Aury had to get out to move larger branches from the path.

Eventually, they spotted the clearing ahead. Scott stopped on the path, just short of the open area.

"Let's cut through the trees here. It looks like it might have once been the path to the front of the building."

They climbed out and grabbed their tools. Aury picked up the black-and-white photo she had taken from the album.

As they approached the building, she held up the photo, comparing it to the squarish overgrowth. She adjusted her approach, trying to match the angles.

"Come look at this and tell me what you think," she said.

Scott joined her and studied the photo. "No, you need to be to your left more." He pointed. "Look at the angle. You shouldn't be able to see the side of the building."

Aury moved into a better position. "Walk closer to the building and to the right more," she directed him.

He did as he was bid.

"A little farther. More to the right. Okay, about there." She tucked the photo into her shirt pocket and hopped and jumped through the kudzu to join him. "Maybe if we shuffle around here a bit, we'll kick something."

Scott laughed. "There is no shuffling in this stuff. You'll have to do it the hard way." He handed her some heavy-duty clippers.

Sighing, she accepted them and went to work chopping at the intrepid vine.

Thirty minutes later, Scott called a halt for a water break. They trudged back to the utility cart for their water bottles.

"What are you going to do with your half of the treasure?" he asked.

"My half? Why would I get anything?"

"We wouldn't be doing this if it weren't for you. It's only fair."

"Don't be ridiculous. This is your land and your treasure," Aury said.

"You've put an awful lot of work into this hunt."

She waved off his comment. "It's been a fun distraction."

"Are you avoiding quilting?" he asked with a playful grin.

She returned his smile. "I'm in a rut, that's all. I took this job to follow my husband—*ex-husband*—and be closer to my grandmother. Don't get me wrong; being closer to her was the best thing I could have done. But the job's not all that exciting. I took it because it was all that was open when I moved here."

"Why not look for something else?"

"Maybe I will. That can be my treasure hunt." She downed the last of her water. "Let's get back to work."

As they neared where they had been cutting, Aury tripped and landed hard, catching herself with her hands.

Scott rushed to her side. "Are you okay?" He helped her to her feet.

She brushed off her hands. "Nothing's broken. I'm just clumsy." She reached for the clippers she had dropped. Then she was on her knees again, pulling at the vines.

"What did you find?"

"Get down here and help me," she said.

Scott started cutting as Aury pulled the ivy taut. In no time, they saw a small, white, stone marker, only six inches off the ground.

"Is that what I think it is?" Aury asked.

Scott felt one flat side, then the other. "I think it has carvings on this side."

Aury scurried around to get a better view. "It's too hard to make out."

"Let's look for more."

Meticulously, they searched the area nearby and only found two more stones, approximately the same height and shape as the first.

"Can you read anything?" Aury asked, staring at the second stone while Scott inspected the third.

"I can't make out anything." He ran his hands over the stone facing. "I can't feel anything either." His disappointment spread to Aury.

She copied his movements and used her hands to inspect the marker closer. "I think this is carved, but I can't make it out."

"I have an idea." He pulled out his cell phone and selected camera. He took his time, taking pictures of both sides of all three stones. "Maybe there'll be more detail when we blow up the image on the computer."

"Good idea. Let's go." Aury was on her feet and heading to the path before Scott had a chance to put his phone away.

They climbed into the utility cart and backtracked to the road, then to Scott's cottage.

Chapter 56

Aury cleaned off the table while Gran put the leftovers away.

"Did you get a hold of the people from Doylestown Library?" Aury asked.

"I did. They were helpful. They even emailed me some files."

"Why don't we call Scott, and you can tell us both at once?"

"Is he in northern Virginia?

Aury nodded. "He's used up most of his vacation time and only makes it down here on weekends." She dried her hands and dialed the phone. When Scott answered, she put him on speaker.

Gran settled herself into a kitchen chair. "I told you I found Pearl's mother, Victoria Townsend, in Doylestown. When Pearl's first husband died, she moved to Doylestown with her mother Victoria. Then Pearl remarried. The research assistant at the library sent me an old newspaper clipping about the wedding. Apparently, the Townsends were high society in that area."

"Mary's diary did say her dad owned a textile factory. Guess that paid well," Aury said.

"Did you find out how Victoria was related to Mary?" Scott asked.

"As a matter of fact, Pearl's grandfather was at the wedding—Frederick Townsend." Gran beamed with pride.

"You did it!" Aury hugged Gran.

"At least we know Frederick survived the Civil War," Scott said.

"Did you find out who Marcus Johnson was?" Aury said.

"Victoria actually had two children who lived to adulthood, Pearl and Marcus."

"But Marcus's name was on the deed for Eastover. Why didn't it pass down his family tree? How did it end up with my great-great-whatever grandmother Pearl?" Scott's confusion was evident through the distance.

"I wondered the same thing," Gran said. "So I checked the death records. Marcus died in 1918 during World War I. The deed was never in Pearl's name and didn't transfer to Matthew Bell Junior—and thus your family line—until much later."

"So it skipped a generation. I wonder why it took so long?" Aury said.

"Maybe because Matthew was only a child at the time. When did you say he was born?" Scott asked.

Gran looked at her notes. "1913."

They each got lost in their own thoughts.

"Looks like I have some more work to do," Gran said. "What about you two? When are we going to get our hands on that treasure?"

Scott laughed. "That's where your granddaughter gets her drive. I plan on being out there again Saturday morning."

"I can meet you if you aren't getting sick of me yet," Aury said.

"Sick of you? No way. That treasure won't get found without you. I'll see you this weekend." Scott said his goodbyes.

Aury had just joined Scott Saturday morning in front of the manor house when Gran's car pulled in. Gran stepped out, followed by a couple in their mid-forties, dressed casually in shorts.

"I have someone I want you to meet." Gran was beaming from ear to ear. "This is Ethan and Joyce Hampton. They're your distant cousins."

Scott gave her a strange look. He offered his hand, introducing himself.

"I was caught off guard as well when Liza called me," Ethan said.

"She does have an energy about her that will make you believe anything though," Joyce said with a grin.

Gran gestured toward the manor house. "Do you think we could sit in the library and talk a while?"

Scott motioned for her to lead the way. He looked at Aury who only shrugged and followed her grandmother up the steps.

Once they were all seated, Gran told her story.

"It didn't make sense to me why Eastover passed to Matthew Bell Jr, but it took so long for his name to show up on the deed. At first, we thought it was because he was only a child, but actually he wasn't granted the deed until 1955 when he was forty-two years old."

"Strange," Aury noted.

"That's what I thought," Gran said. "So I did some digging in the court records in Doylestown."

Ethan and Joyce smiled and waited patiently. They apparently already knew this part.

"When Pearl remarried, her second husband, Daniel Cartwright, was none too happy that her seven-year-old son, Matthew Junior, inherited a piece of land he felt should be his."

"Daniel was my great-great-grandfather," Ethan offered.

"It wasn't until Matthew Junior had a son who was getting married that it got settled. He had to fight his stepfather in court to get the deed in his name so he could give it to his son Grant when he got married."

"My grandfather?" Scott asked.

"One and the same," Gran said.

"But how did you get caught up in this?" Scott asked Ethan.

Gran replied for him. "I tracked Pearl's children from her second marriage. There were a lot more leads on that side of the family, and Doylestown isn't that big. It didn't take long to trace the branches to Ethan's family. When I told him about you, he was excited to pay a visit."

"We were due for a getaway, so we jumped at the chance. I hope you don't mind," Ethan said.

Scott smiled. "Of course not. Where did you come in from?"

"Ithaca, New York," Joyce said.

"Isn't that where Cornell University is?" Aury said.

Joyce nodded. "I teach in the computer engineering college there."

"And we own a vineyard on Seneca Lake," Ethan added.

"I'll bet it's beautiful." Aury smiled.

"You'll have to come for a visit sometime," Joyce offered.

"We've been meaning to make it down to Virginia for ages. I'm glad we finally had an excuse," Ethan said.

"We've heard so many stories over the years that we couldn't pass up a chance to see this place," Joyce said.

Ethan jumped in. "Great-grandpa Cartwright—that would be Pearl's son—used to tell us about how *his* ancestors supported the Union during the Civil War, even though they lived in Virginia. There's quite the legend about how two young boys and their little sister made their way through the Confederate lines to Pennsylvania with only a donkey cart, three slaves, and their wits."

"You'd think they fought off half the Confederate soldiers to hear the old folks tell it," Joyce said.

"Guess it's been embellished over the years." Ethan took Joyce's hand.

She smiled at him. "But to see where it all started is fascinating."

"I'm lost," Scott admitted. "I've never heard this story."

"Really? I would've thought you heard the same tale. It's an annual reenactment at our family reunion," Ethan said.

"It's not quite that bad," Joyce assured him. "But I could

recite it in my sleep."

"My family tree is thin, and many died young during the wars. I'd be lonely at a family reunion."

"Please tell us the story," Aury said.

Ethan sat back into the couch and gazed into the empty fireplace, gathering his thoughts.

"During the Civil War, Eastover was a simple farm owned by James and Mary Townsend," he began.

"We found Mary's diaries," Aury jumped in.

"I'd love to read them," Joyce said.

"After the story. I'm dying to hear this legend," Scott said.

"Well, seems like James disappeared, along with his eldest son. No one knows what happened to them." Ethan went on to fill in the blanks about Mary's life as well as her five children. It tracked with what Scott and Aury had pieced together.

When he got to the part about the three slaves meeting the children, Aury was on the edge of her seat.

"The ruse they cooked up about the slaves being charged to take the kids north worked well. They were stopped and checked a few times, but Thomas or Emily would turn on the tears, and the soldiers let them pass, probably so they wouldn't get stuck with whiney kids." Ethan stretched his long legs out in front of him and considered his toes.

"The legend says the kids' grandparents were so happy, they gave the three men jobs in the factory. The parents never showed up though."

"I wonder why I never heard this story," Scott mused again.

"Your family tree is down Matthew Bell's side. Senior died before his son was more than a toddler. He didn't have a chance to pass on many stories," Gran said.

"But Matthew's mother could have told him. After all, it was her family legend."

"Could just be timing, being in the right place at the right time," Joyce said. "Maybe Junior wasn't around when the grandparents were passing on the stories. His half-siblings were quite a few years behind him."

"Did they say anything about the treasure?" Aury asked.

"What treasure?" Joyce said.

"We've been following clues Mary left to find something hidden. It started as a game for the kids, so it could be nothing at all," Scott said.

"Or it could be something," Aury insisted. "Sarah left a note for Thomas saying she was going to hide something valuable."

"We don't know if he ever found it," Scott said.

"What kind of clues?" Joyce asked.

"We find a short poem or note, and it takes us to another location where we dig up another clue. We've found . . ." He turned to Aury. "Six, so far?"

Aury counted them in her head. "Yes. But I think we're close."

Gran watched the exchange with sheer delight. "I'm so glad you all got to meet each other. This has been such a wonderful day."

Aury slapped Scott playfully on the leg. "You have cousins!"

"You have a lot of cousins," Ethan said. "I have three sisters, three sets of aunts and uncles—and they all have kids—and my grandma was one of four."

"Do they all live in Pennsylvania?" Gran asked.

"Mostly Pennsylvania, Maryland, and New York."

"Wow! I can't imagine a family reunion with that many people," Scott said.

"That's only one branch. I'll have to sketch it out for you."

"That would be great. Between Aury and Liza, I have learned more about my past than I ever thought possible."

"So what are you going to do with the treasure?" Joyce asked.

Scott shrugged. "If one even exists, it would be great to have enough money to keep this camp running like my parents would have liked."

"Liza told us your parents died young. I'm sorry to hear that," Ethan offered.

"Thanks. And we recently got hit with a hurricane that took

out the motel. It's taking me a while to get back on my feet."

"The commute isn't helping either," Aury said.

Ethan and Joyce looked at Scott.

"I live in northern Virginia. I'm fixing up this place on the weekends," he explained.

"That's rough. I don't suppose you could take over Eastover full time?" Joyce said.

"I'm running the numbers and considering it."

"I understand where you're coming from," Ethan said. "It was a scary leap to buy the vineyard and give up my day job. But I tell you what, I love the outdoors and the people who walk through my door. They come from everywhere, and they all have a different story."

Aury smiled at Scott. "That's what I've been telling him."

Chapter 57

T hat was a good visit," Aury commented after Gran, Ethan, and Joyce had departed.

Scott looked at his watch. "But we are way behind schedule. I need to switch over the cottages. I have two more families coming in tonight."

"I'll help. Then we can go to the church."

"I have to stop by the campsites and make sure everything looks good there as well."

"I can't believe you have campers already," Aury said as she and Scott piled into the utility cart.

"It was a great idea. I started getting hits almost as soon as I put it on the website. I also listed it with some of the tourist sites and now I'm booked out through early October."

"And I see the temporary bridge was replaced."

"Yep. I needed to prioritize that so the contractors could move their equipment back here to start tearing down the motel."

After they finished cleaning and changing out the linens in the two rentable cottages, they stopped by Scott's cottage for water.

"What did you want to show me?" Aury asked.

Scott opened a folder he had sitting on the table and pulled out three photographs printed on full sheets of paper. "These are the white stones we found. I had a friend from the office run them through a program he had to make the markings more distinct."

Aury picked up the pages, studying them closely. "He did a great job. I can't believe how much detail he found."

"Two of them were definitely carved with dates. The third one doesn't have any markings he could detect."

"November 2, 1847, through November 21, 1847. How sad." She flipped to the next one. "Emma Grace April 12, 1854, through December 23, 1856. It's bad enough to lose a child, but to lose one right before Christmas had to be tough on the whole family."

She stared at the next photo, holding it close, then farther away from her eyes. "You're right. I don't see anything on this."

Scott said, "There's one more page because he tried to sharpen the detail from both sides."

Aury repeated the process but gave up and shook her head. "Why bother marking a grave without a carving?"

"Could be they didn't have a chance to complete the carving before having to leave," Scott suggested.

"Or that could be where the treasure is buried!"

"Did you bring your metal detector?"

"It's in the trunk of my car."

They wasted no time retrieving the metal detector and bumping their way down the uneven path to the old church. The sun had reached its zenith and was working its way back down the sky.

Scott grabbed a shovel and clippers while Aury gathered her metal detector and headset. After clearing the vines away from the white, unmarked stone, Scott stepped aside to give Aury access. She flipped a switch and began a sweeping motion across the ground.

As he waited, Scott wandered around the side of the church. "Aury!" After no response, he called again. "Hey, Aury!"

Aury looked up. Seeing Scott staring at her, she removed the headset. "What's up?"

"Come check this out."

She followed him around the building to where he had hacked away at a swath of kudzu close to the ground.

Peeking through the dark green, Aury saw several small, white stones, very similar to what they had found out front.

She shook her head in frustration. "Do you think they're more grave markers?"

"Could be. Or they may have collected them for another reason and used a few to mark the graves because they were handy."

"Why couldn't this be simple?"

"Were you picking up anything?" Scott asked, indicating the metal detector.

"A little but I'm not sure."

"How do we know we won't be adding to your bottle cap collection?"

"We don't. This isn't a high-end model where you can set for different metals. It's a simple yes or no."

"Why don't you try it over the marked graves and see if there's a difference?" he suggested.

"Good idea."

They returned to the front of the building, and Aury began sweeping across a larger area. Finally she took off the headset and handed the equipment to Scott.

"It sounds the same to me," she said.

Scott repeated her process and confirmed there was no significant jump in the signal.

"I don't want to dig up a coffin," Aury said.

"Neither do I."

"How deep do you think coffins are buried?"

"Isn't the saying 'six feet under'?" Scott glanced at the sky. It was getting dark although it wasn't even four o'clock yet.

"If a young girl were to bury a treasure, she probably wouldn't dig that far. A couple feet at the most, I would think. Especially depending on how big the container was." Aury picked up the shovel from where Scott had put it aside. She resolutely plunged it into the soil near the unmarked stone. A rumble of thunder accompanied her movement.

While she dug, Scott investigated the front of the church building. Chopping away some weeds, he located the front door, it's once-beautiful wood now a mix of black and green spores from mold and ivy. Tearing away enough of the kudzu to reach the handle and clear a barely-man-sized opening, Scott was excited to see what was inside.

"I found something!" Aury called.

Scott joined her, dropping to his knees to pull out dirt with his hands.

The first drop of rain hit Aury's face. "Uh-oh." She fell to her knees also and began to dig beside Scott.

As water fell from the sky, the freshly dug ground turned to mud, sliding back to fill the hole as quickly as they could scoop it out.

"We can't give up now," Aury said. "We're too close."

Lightning lit the sky. Scott doubled his efforts. He slipped his fingers under a wooden box the size of a breadbox. "See if you can clear away the other end."

Aury dug furiously, leaning over the hole to block the onslaught of rain. "Got it."

"Now pull—hard!"

Together they struggled with the case until the suction of the mud released and the box popped free of the hole. Aury landed on her backside, laughing. Scott grabbed the box and made a dash for the church door.

Aury followed him. He handed over the box to her. "Hold this. I'm going to see if I can open this door."

He stepped on top of the ivy at the bottom of the door to increase the opening size. With his hand on the latch, he pressed down at the same time as pushing on the door with his shoulder. After a few progressively harder strikes, the door gave way, propelling him through the door, tripping as his foot caught in the ivy.

Aury was through the door in a flash, jumping nimbly over

Scott. She set the box down and rushed to shut the door behind them, blocking out the gale force winds that had kicked up with the storm.

As she pulled the damp hair out of her eyes, she looked around the dark space. The only light entering was from the two windows she and Scott had uncovered when they visited before. With the storm outside, even that light was too weak to do them much good.

Scott sneezed.

"Bless you," she said.

He stood and took stock. "This place is a mess." He tried to wipe his hands on his pants but only succeeded in making more mud.

A sudden whooshing noise caused Aury to duck as something flew past her head and landed in the rafters.

"Well, that's one more problem to deal with," Scott muttered.

Aury laughed at herself. "But at least we're out of the rain."

"It came on so suddenly. I have a feeling it will blow through."

"What's in the box?" Aury asked.

Scott picked it up and took it to a table closer to the windows at the back of the church. When he set it down, it kicked up another flurry of dust. It was Aury's turn to sneeze multiple times.

"Bless *you!*" Scott said with a laugh.

Leaning in close, he examined the latch holding the box closed.

"Wait. I have a light." Aury pulled out her phone and turned on the flashlight.

Even through the mud, they could see a beautifully sculpted wooden box. Aury ran her fingers across the carved images on the lid.

Scott studied the latch. Standing, he said, "Let me borrow your phone a minute."

He took the light and shone it around the open room until

he found what he was looking for. He picked up a thin stick and worked to clear away the mud from the mechanism.

Finally they were rewarded with a click as the clasp came free.

"Ready for this?" Scott asked.

"Do you think it's the treasure or another clue?"

"It better be the treasure after all this."

He lifted the lid, and Aury shone the light inside. The glint off golden metal was bright and shiny.

Chapter 58

I s that what I think it is?" Aury said.

Scott picked up two of the gold coins, turning them back and forth in the light. Replacing them, he pulled out a heavy package wrapped in cloth. Holding it in the palm of his hand, he unwrapped a sparkling necklace made of sapphires and diamonds.

"Oh, my!" Aury said.

Scott handed it to her and reached in for another bag. He loosened the drawstrings and tipped two pairs of earrings into his hand.

Aury was overwhelmed by the beauty of the jewelry as Scott pulled yet another bag from the chest.

More stones glittered in the flashlight, having been protected from dust by the cloth they were encased in. This necklace wouldn't have been worn on a farm during any time period. The teardrop red jewel was surrounded by chips of blue sparkles.

"I can't believe it's really a treasure," she said. She picked up a locket, elegantly engraved with roses hanging on a thin gold chain. She held the phone under her chin as she used her thumbnails to pry open the two-inch pendant. Inside, a very happy couple was pictured in their wedding finery. The man stood tall with one hand resting on the shoulder of his seated bride. Aury closed the locket, saying a silent prayer for the couple.

Coins clicked together as Scott counted them out. "Twenty. I wonder what they're worth?"

When they finished searching the box, they had found the locket, three other necklaces, four pairs of earrings, twenty gold coins, and a stack of papers. Scott decided to wait until they got to his cottage to sort through them.

They put everything neatly back into the box and closed the lid. Only then did they notice the pounding rain had stopped. The wind still blew in the trees, occasionally throwing a shower of raindrops from the nearby leaves.

As light slowly crept into the room through the windows, Aury was able to take in her surroundings. The table they were using to support the box was likely the altar. A moth-ridden, once-white cloth was draped across the top and reached almost to the floor.

A beautiful cross decorated the table, carved in dark wood and standing erect on a marble stand. Scott went to inspect the chairs facing the altar. He ran his hand across the grimy surface.

"These are beautiful. If they've been here since Mary's day, they're antiques," he said.

"Look at this stained-glass window."

Scott looked at the four-foot square pane leaning against the wall. "They must have been waiting to put this in one of the windows."

When Aury shone her flashlight on it, the light picked up on the many colors pulling together a pastoral scene ending on a high hill. Even with the dirt, she could tell it was a work of art.

Aury shone the light into a corner of the room where she noticed a pile of junk. Upon closer inspection, she made out a large, square object covered with a horse blanket buried underneath old wood crates and extra pieces of lumber.

"Help me clear this off," she said.

She and Scott removed the items stacked on top and pulled on the heavy blanket, letting it fall to the floor revealing a trunk with leather latches, deteriorated with age.

"Mary's diary said they were going to move some of their valuables to hide them from passing soldiers. You don't suppose this is it, do you?"

Scott lifted the lid. Lovingly packed inside were elegant dishes, silver candlesticks, small paintings, and a few hand-carved toys. More things were packed another layer underneath.

Aury picked up a wooden horse. "This was probably special to one of the kids, and they didn't want anything to happen to it."

"I guess if they decided they had to leave in a hurry, these were things they couldn't take with them, but they didn't want anyone else to have them either."

Aury spread her arms to take in the room. "Scott, the things in this room are a treasure in themselves. I'll bet you have enough here to fix up Eastover—not counting the stuff in the box!"

A bright smile broke across Scott's face. He rushed to Aury and swept her off her feet, spinning her in circles.

Chapter 59

A Year Later

Aury watched as Scott floated between groups, a handshake here, a quick hug there. He looked happy and in his element.

The official opening day of Eastover's new motel had gone brilliantly, with press and government representation to cut the ribbon. *The advertising will serve him well*, Aury thought.

It helped that Eastover was already booked to capacity between the new lodge, the manor house, and the campsites. Scott had been able to sell off enough items from the church to make the repairs while still keeping the more precious items in his family.

Ethan's suggestion to hold the next Spencer family reunion in Virginia was met with an overwhelming response. Everyone wanted to see the place where the legend started.

This year, they called it the Spencer-Bell family reunion, tying together both sides of Pearl Townsend Bell Spencer's family.

Scott slumped into a lawn chair at Aury's side. "Who knew family could be so exhausting?"

She bumped him with her shoulder. "You love it."

"I do." His face was bright with a smile. "Thanks for coming out today. It's probably not much fun for you with a bunch of strangers, but it's going to be your family soon." He picked up her hand and kissed it. "This wouldn't have come together without you and Liza." He looked around. "Where is she, by the way?"

Aury nodded in the direction of the dessert table where Gran was dishing out food. "She's never met a stranger. Besides, she likes to help."

"That's obvious enough. Has she made any progress on your genealogy?"

This time, Aury laughed out loud. "She has transformed her living room into a work area. She puts stickies on everything and purchased a flip chart where she can make diagrams and then sticks those to the walls."

"Why doesn't she use the computer?"

"She still prefers old-school research. She looks things up on the computer but wants to see the results large enough to refer to when she needs it. I have a feeling it will be up to me to pull everything together when she's finished."

"There you are!" Ethan's hearty voice reached them from behind.

"Come join us," Aury offered with a wave.

Ethan took the seat next to Scott. "Now are you sorry you discovered family?"

Scott returned his smile. "Not at all. I love having everyone here. It's been great."

"This may become the go-to spot for our future reunions. Be careful what you wish for. Aury, show me this ring Joyce's been going on about."

Aury held up the platinum, filigree, engagement ring featuring a square-cut diamond. "Scott found it among the hidden treasure."

Ethan took the time to admire the craftsmanship. "Congratulations, you two. I expect an invite to the wedding."

"Absolutely," Scott said. "Did I tell you the Virginia War Museum is going to display Mary's jewelry and coins in a traveling exhibit? The American Civil War Center in Richmond is putting it together," Scott said.

"That's wonderful," Ethan said.

"They may even do a video retelling the Townsend legend to go along with it."

"You're famous!"

"Honestly, I'd settle for the marketing and bookings that will hopefully come from the exhibit. But they're offering me a stipend for the loan of the items."

Two towhead youths about ten and eleven ran up to Scott's chair. "Will you show us the haunted woods?"

Scott cut Aury a look as she stifled a grin.

"Of course. Why don't we wait until after dinner though?" Scott replied.

"But before dark," Aury added. "Scott doesn't like going into the woods when it's dark."

The kids jumped up and down in excitement and ran off to tell the others.

"Thanks for revealing my weakness," Scott said.

"Oh, they don't see it as a weakness. To them, it will make the adventure that much more realistic."

Scott rested his head on the back of the chair. "The restoration of the church is coming along nicely. It'll be a while before it's open to the public, but the kudzu is mostly gone. Treating it over the summer made the difference. It was easier to cut once the vines started dying."

They sat watching the people, young and old, gathered in small groups chattering away. In the distance, someone played a guitar. Kids kicked a soccer ball in and around the lawn chairs.

"Take that ball out to the field," Gran said from her station by the food. "We don't need you tripping folks."

Aury shook her head while Scott and Ethan laughed.

"She fits in well." Ethan turned to address Scott and Aury directly. "Joyce and I would love it if you came to visit us in Ithaca. I think you'd enjoy the vineyard."

"Definitely," Scott replied before Aury had a chance to.

She cut him a look with raised eyebrows. "As long as we get a wine tasting out of it," Aury said to Ethan.

"Are you kidding? I'm going to teach you how to prepare your own mix of grapes."

"I'll bring some bottles here to offer in the manor house."

Ethan agreed. "I'm thinking you two might be able to help me with my own little mystery."

Aury's curiosity was piqued. "Do you have a hidden treasure too?"

"I wish. No, but there's a rumor in town that the mixing room is haunted."

"By someone who drowned in a vat?" Scott asked.

"That's gross." Aury gave his arm a light punch.

"We're not sure, but I don't think it was in a vat. Those are fairly new and enclosed. I'll tell you the whole story when you come up. I don't want to scare you off just yet."

"Sounds like a challenge. We'll set something up," Scott said.

Epilogue

Aury sat on the wooden porch surrounding the lodge. The music of the wildlife in the nearby woods was soothing. She thought about the last time she had sat here. Glancing at the sky, she saw no clouds and could easily even make out the faint glow of the moon in the evening twilight.

When the chilly breeze picked up, she wrapped her sweater tighter around her and rose from her seat. As she opened the door to the meeting space, the wave of sound rolled over her. Voices and laughter from the many quilters working diligently at their machines or gathered around a partially finished project to offer suggestions were music to her ears.

Stopping by the snack table, she grabbed a cookie, then on second thought, picked up another one. When she reached her workstation, she held out one of the cookies to her gran. The older woman looked up from her hand stitching.

"Oatmeal. My favorite," Gran said.

"What are you working on?" Aury asked.

"I thought Scott would appreciate a reminder of this adventure." Gran held up a label decorated with lilacs. It read:

> *In dedication to Eastover Retreat Center*
> *I'll give you concealed treasures and riches*
> *hidden in secret places, so that you'll know that*

it is I, the Lord, the God of Israel, who calls you
by name. - *Isaiah 45:3*

From the Colonial Piecemakers Quilt Guild
September 2025

"It's perfect!" Aury said.

"We have a ta-da!" Debbie announced, silencing the room.

Pat and Carla held the fabric in the upper corners and let it unfold to reach the floor.

The quilt was a beautiful combination of colors accentuated by the detailed applique of a building closely resembling the lodge in which they sat. A golden cross gleamed from above the front doors, and the yellow fabric used to form the windows glowed. Looking closely, Aury picked up on the dark clouds in the distance although the sky was clear in the foreground.

The greens and yellows around the bottom edges made Aury feel as if she were looking through the bushes at the lodge. As she stepped closer, she saw where the ladies had quilted leaf shapes over the area indicating the lawn leading up to the front door.

This representation perfectly captured the warmth and affection that was Eastover. Scott was going to love it.

########

If you have enjoyed *Eastover Treasures*, we would love a review on whatever platform you are most comfortable with.

https://books2read.com/EastoverTreasures

Acknowledgements

Nothing comes together without an excellent team, but a few deserve a special shout out.

Special thanks to Michael L. Blakey, Ph.D.
National Endowment for the Humanities Professor
of Anthropology, Africana Studies, and American Studies
Director of the Institute for Historical Biology
College of William & Mary

Janet Hopkins
Senior Laboratory Specialist
College of William & Mary

My Beta Readers, Brenda Barden,
Amy Voltaire, author of *My Name is Erin and My Mom's an Addict,* and
Vikki Lynn Smith, author of the In the Woods children's book series.

and

My wonderful editor who teaches me something new every time, Narielle Living, author of *Signs of the South, Revenge of the Past*, and *Madness in Brewster Square*

Free Quilt Pattern

D uring COVID-19, I spent a lot of time catching up on my quilting. Without the ability to get new fabric, I set a goal of making as many things as I could from scraps. After hundreds of masks, I switched to scrap quilts.

This is a fun one because the colors don't need to match, you can make almost any size, and the outcome lends to an impressive 3D appearance.

The width of the strips doesn't matter, although they should be parallel for the best effect.

1. Gather strips that are at least 4.5" long. They can vary, but I recommend putting the longest ones together if possible, to save time on your sewing.

2. Sew together on the long side, making a semi-straight edge on the top (you will trim to make it exact later). Sew as many strips as you want to work with at one time. You can add more later or sew multiple smaller groups of strips together to make them easier to handle.

3. Press all the seams the same way.

4. Turn and cut into 4.5" strips perpendicular to your sewing lines.

5. With whatever you have left over, you can start another row of strips.

6. When you have enough blocks for the size quilt you want, do the following:

7. Place two blocks together face-to-face with the strips going the SAME DIRECTION. That's very important.

8. On the back of one, draw a line corner to corner. Sew 1/4"
on either side of the line.

9. Cut on the line.

10. Press.

11. Trim to 4" squares, ensuring to line up your ruler so the
center seam is exactly on the corners.

12. Lay your blocks using the pattern below. Every other row
has the same pattern. You can start and stop at any size, and it
doesn't change the impact.

13. Press the seams for the rows in alternating directions to
reduce the bulk (ie., row one, all to the right; row two, all to the
left).

14. Sew the rows together, careful to nest the block seams.
Press.

15. Add a solid thin border. Size will vary depending on the size of your quilt.

16. You can add another larger border (approx. twice the size as the thin) that's a solid color or you can get creative with your scraps. Take what's left of your strips sewn together and cut the width of your border to create railroad tracks. Or cut them at an angle for a different effect. Or you could even make crumb squares and turn it into a border.

Scrap quilts are also great for practicing quilting on your home machine.

Have fun!

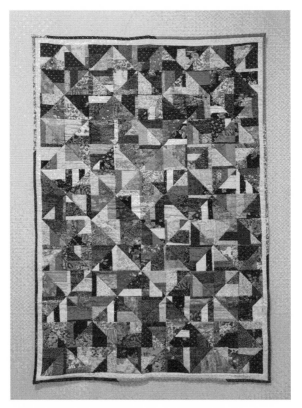

Visit my website to see the final quilt in color.

https://DawnBrothertonAuthor.com